Between Rothko and 3 Windows

Between Rothko and 3 Windows
Murder at the Art Gallery of Ontario

Corrado Paina

Translated from the Italian
by Damiano Pietropaolo

QUATTRO BOOKS

Copyright © 2016 Corrado Paina and Quattro Books Inc.

The use of any part of this publication, reproduced, transmitted in any form or by any means, electronic, mechanical, photocopying, or otherwise stored in an electronic retrieval system without the prior consent (as applicable) of the individual author, artist or the designer, is an infringement of the copyright law.

The publication of *Between Rothko and 3 Windows* has been generously supported by the Canada Council for the Arts and the Ontario Arts Council.

Canada Council for the Arts / Conseil des arts du Canada

ONTARIO ARTS COUNCIL
CONSEIL DES ARTS DE L'ONTARIO
an Ontario government agency
un organisme du gouvernement de l'Ontario

Author Photo: Deborah Verginella
Cover design: Natasha Shaikh
Typography: Diane Mascherin

Library and Archives Canada Cataloguing in Publication

Paina, Corrado, 1954-
[Tra Rothko e tre finestre. English]
    Between Rothko and 3 windows / Corrado Paina ; Damiano Pietropaolo, translator.

Translation of: Tra Rothko e tre finestre.
ISBN 978-1-988254-36-4 (paperback)

    I. Pietropaolo, Damiano, translator II. Title. III. Title: Tra Rothko e tre finestre. English.

PS8581.A484T7313 2016   C853'.92   C2016-906375-5

Published by Quattro Books Inc.
Toronto
info@quattrobooks.ca
www.quattrobooks.ca

Printed in Canada

Prologue
College Street

On that particular day the ATM room at the bank reeked with the odour of the young Brazilian tramp. He would sleep there overnight and leave at the crack of dawn to avoid being caught by the police and arrested. It was six in the morning and, as he did each day, Luigi Sasta went down to College Street for a coffee and a newspaper. He stepped into the bank to get some cash. The young Brazilian's odour was almost pleasant, familiar, different from the stench of the Portuguese drunk who babbled away in every language, and had once been a professor, maybe even an academic authority, in an institution in some faraway world, alien to Canada.

The Portuguese had not been seen for a while. Last summer Luigi had talked a cop out of throwing him in jail, explaining to him that the old guy was harmless, that he was from the mainland, not the islands – the old man was keen on people knowing that he was not from the Azores. He was back again making the rounds of the cafés only to ask for some loose change for which he would speak in some foreign language or recite some important quotation that would rise up in his mind from the liquid chaos of his past.

At times, giving in to his passion, he would rant in anger against all the people from the Azores, thousands, who lived on and around College Street. According to the old Portuguese they were nothing but a herd of illiterate peasants, and he would rail against the regulars from the Azores for calling the police instead of raging against him. But thanks to

Luigi's intervention he had not been arrested, and the cop had even stopped short of giving him a pep talk.

The old guy had moved away along the sidewalk without even thanking him, not that Luigi expected any gratitude. Soon he stopped to gaze with his vacant and watery eyes at the falling snow and the streetcar rattling its way into the storm. College Street has changed, we have changed, Luigi thought to himself. The fauna of the street has changed. Turned to plastic, it's all clean and beautiful. The owners of the new restaurants are not from the neighbourhood; their only goal is to strike it rich. They are only here to turn a quick profit; they have no sense of commitment to the community, no sense of belonging. The new shopkeepers and their clients did not know the tramps and the homeless of the street, had not watched them grow old. They found them aggravating, an inconvenience, and so they called the police.

On cold winter nights the young Brazilian and the old Portuguese waited for the last customer to open the heavy doors of the bank's ATM room with his convenience card, followed him inside and waited politely until he left before laying down to sleep: children of the sea and of green hills seeking shelter from the Canadian cold. They would remove their shoes and place them beside their makeshift bedding next to the plastic cups they used to beg for spare change. The old, drunk Portuguese would fall asleep as soon as he hit the floor. In the last few years, if truth were told, the bank left the doors to the ATM room open overnight. Luigi smiled, thinking that it must have been a conscious decision taken by compassionate bank workers.

In the early morning customers in need of cash walked in without fear and went about their transactions calmly, lulled by the snoring sound of the old guy gurgling like a fountain while the young man slept like a baby, his nose and cheek flattened against a makeshift pillow.

Between Rothko and 3 Windows

From time to time a black man sporting a huge mane of dreadlocks made his appearance, talking to himself until he collapsed from exhaustion. A client would walk in, but he would continue the low rumble-drone of his untranslatable, never-ending rosary. On College Street no one was afraid, not even of him.

Around six o'clock or shortly after Tony would go to sleep in the basement of his Italian café. Everyone knew that he waited till then because two or three of his girls would be leaving the place, just in time before the morning regulars came in for their coffee. The old barista raised the metal shutters to let them in, swearing at Tony and his sluts, cursing with even more anger the powder that Tony preferred over the girls.

The silence of College Street was broken by the girls' noisy exit. Dishevelled and worn out by sleep, they walked out, hailing a taxi, their shrill voices echoing along the street with its bars and cafés still closed. The first morning streetcar had started on its loop. Older Italian immigrants, who still felt that they owned College Street – though less and less these days – walked about waiting for the café to open so they could enjoy a real coffee, made the only way it should be.

They had never gotten used to the espresso at the Portuguese bar, the only one to remain open for business overnight. There, they could find an old man who had worked as a miner in Belgium, another one who had become obsessed with Padre Pio, and the pizza maker, who was now retired but still worked part-time, as his pizza was still the best one around. He would go to the pizzeria around three or four in the morning, prepare the dough and return to College Street. They took their seats, somewhat self-consciously, at the Portuguese bar, which at this time was teeming with labourers and small construction contractors silently sipping their coffee, while waiting for the Italian café to open because, even at this hour, although it was illegal, there they could order a coffee laced with grappa from what looked like a water bottle next to the espresso machine.

On leaving the Portuguese café, the old immigrants braced against the Canadian chill by walking back and forth on College. There was always something to argue about, but on seeing the girls leaving Tony's bar, their gaze of old peasants who had become urbanized against their will veiled over with sadness. They looked on quietly at the girls walking away unsteady on their feet, drowsy with the after-effects of drugs, their shrill voices fading. They looked on them with the weary eyes of those who have been around the world, only they had not really been around the world, they had merely crossed it.

These girls reminded them of the girls who had gone to visit them in the shacks – in Switzerland ... in Belgium? Maybe they were the same girls speaking the same incomprehensible language they had spoken thirty or forty years ago; now, they haunted construction sites or even well-lit neighbourhoods in downtown Toronto.

"She could be our daughter!"

"Your mean granddaughter," the pizza man corrected him.

"They're so young," sighed the miner.

"And that good-for-nothing left his family ... his wife and children ..."

The old man who was obsessed with Padre Pio was from Calabria and was uncharacteristically very chatty in contrast to other older men who met every afternoon, year in, year out, day in, day out, at the Caravella social club. He always went on longer that he should, speaking words out of turn about someone from the neighbourhood. And he spoke with contempt, as well. Tony was lacking in honour ... maybe even more ... maybe he was a criminal.

Word got around that Tony might have spilled too much to the police, and the Mafia had forced him into house arrest in the cellar of his own bar where he spent his time sniffing cocaine and entertaining half-wasted girls he would pump full of drugs.

Stories of College Street ... small stories ... true stories ... stories that will never become legends ... coffee house gossip ... telltale anecdotes of people who knew each other well.

Luigi thought of another College Street, that of the shoemaker and his friends who gathered to speak of revolution. Every morning they met in the shoe shop to comment on the Italian language daily, conspiring to create subversive scenarios – something they had started when they were young immigrants, but that now had become a tradition. The shoemaker had given them notice that he would soon be closing the shop. The landlord was raising the rent, and had promised the space to the neighbouring restaurant looking to expand.

Luigi left the house early in the morning, stopping to buy a newspaper, drink his coffee, smoke a couple of du Mauriers, and listen for a while to the gossip. Occasionally he took part in it, but more often than not he simply offered his much sought-after opinion before taking his leave to return home and get ready for work. He was always ready for anything that would take his mind off the *Stampa Italica*, the Italian language daily of which he was the editor and director – the unfinished articles, the on-going investigations, his relationship with the publisher, the chronic lack of money.

About a year and a half ago, as he had been leaving the newsstand that sold the *Corriere della Sera*, the *Corriere dello Sport*, the *Gazzetta*, *Oggi*, *Tex Willer* and *Diabolik*, he had felt an acute discomfort in his chest, followed by a great shiver, an agonizing, arresting pain creeping up his shoulders and neck, and he had been overcome by a wretched fear of dying on the spot.

He had lost his balance right there on the threshold and had been helped up by three older men, who took him to the bar next door, offering him some water rather than the usual coffee. The owner of the newsstand and his wife had rushed to him as well. An old immigrant from Venezuela had helped him into his Cadillac and taken him to the emergency room. A couple of days later he had been let go, and his daughter Elena had come to pick him up.

"It was nothing," Luigi had said, wanting to reassure her, "just a minor discomfort." Old age creeping in, he had said, trying to play down what had happened.

"So why don't you just stop working and retire," she had insisted.

Easier said than done, Luigi thought.

Luigi insisted that it was just an incident brought on by the draft. It had been a very cold day. But he knew very well that it was angina, as the resident doctor in the hospital had diagnosed.

And the wretched angina got worse and worse.

Chapter 1

Michele Carrieri always left the building during his lunch break, never ate his meal in the office, and his colleagues considered him a snob because of it. He also found a polite excuse every time they invited him out for a sandwich or salad at the Grange, a cramped mall that had kept the name of the old location of the Gallery of Modern Art. Hundreds of office workers gathered like ravenous herds in the Grange (which means cattle-shed or stable), chirping away as they took their seats under a low ceiling that gave the place the look of an A-bomb shelter with bare electrical wires criss-crossing like frantic eels in an enclosed pond. Here they slurped away on vegetable soups, chomped on frigid salads.

The mere thought of having to spend another four hours at his workstation in the office reinforced Michele's preference for the large table in the archives room. It was less squalid there, even in the garish glow of its neon lights, its dusty collection of old commercial directories and price lists, than to have to listen to his colleagues chatter on about mortgage rates, their next vacation on some beach in Varadero or the accomplishments of their growing children. During the twelve-thirty lunch break, packed in an elevator, they ticked off the floor numbers in silence, humming away at some little tune like schoolchildren in a hurry, catching in the cabin's mirror reflections of familiar faces, semblances of humanity. One of Michele's colleagues, originally from Italy, approached him, asking if he was following the World Cup.

Michele, with the barest hint of a smile, replied with chilly politeness that he was not a fan of soccer. He almost regretted his answer, but then he thought that it was rather hypocritical that their only moment of national solidarity should find concrete expression in a soccer championship, cheering for a team in a faraway country. Did they have nothing else in common?

The cabin doors opened, offering Michele the opportunity to take flight. The sun smacked him in the face. The city, that nucleus of great buildings that Robert Ford Gagen had labelled the temples of commerce, shimmered in the sunlight. The tall, glassy skyscrapers were veiled over with liquid gold. Offices, computers, files, employees disappeared behind the great wave of sunlight. The long winter was finally over, and the wind that forced pedestrians into the frigid embrace of the great insurance companies' buildings and skyscrapers had died down.

According to the weather forecasts Michele remembered from listening to CBC radio in his bathroom, the temperature would surge above thirty degrees with a very high humidity index. He had decided to wear, for the last time, his grey wool challis suit. In the past few days summer had exploded without even a hint of a springtime break. The city was afloat in the sultry heat wave.

"This land is not fit for human beings, only for animals," an Italian immigrant had once told him on a winter's morning. The two of them had been approaching from opposite directions, dragging themselves on the sidewalks of Little Italy, covering their eyes and faces with their scarves, offering what resistance they could against the blast of the oncoming storm. Michele never did figure out how the old man could recognize him as an Italian; he had watched him make his way as he had vomited his words towards him, had seen him pull his head down into his shoulders before disappearing in the grey vortex. To be sure, a steely constitution was necessary to withstand the assault of such extreme changes in weather. Winter and summer temperatures could alternate from one day to the next. Michele had grown accustomed to these changes but was unable to predict what was coming tomorrow, and so he failed, once again, to put away his winter clothing.

As he walked towards the café for the usual panino, he remembered that he had no money, and turned back towards the bank next door to his office. He crossed Dundas Street, skirting the monument to fallen airmen in the world wars, a porous clay cement *mehnir* whose outstretched arms seemed to release into freedom a bird that resembled an airplane.

At the base of this monument reaching up to the heavens, a homeless person had frozen to death this past winter. People walked by in a hurry but sometimes, remembering the poor old tramp, they stopped to place bunches of flowers on the spot. Michele loosened his tie, and gave his last remaining change to a teenaged boy sitting on the steps of the bank, shaking wildly and scratching his head.

He pushed open the heavy glass door that led into a dark vault, where automatic banking machines stood waiting like altars from the early Christian era. Their electronic beeping broke the silence, marking the liturgy of banking transactions performed in silence by wary customers. Michele had little money in his account and withdrew only a twenty-dollar bill. For a brief moment he thought the screen of the automatic teller would refuse his request, but the bill appeared and Michele grabbed it with childlike joy. When he left the bank, another beggar stopped him, asking for money, grumbling that he needed a bed. Michele told him he had no change only to be yelled at, called a liar and spat upon. Still shaken, Michele took out his handkerchief to wipe the sleeve of his jacket, and the beggar moved on, crying out against a woman who skilfully avoided him and even more skilfully avoided the gob aimed at her. Michele did not feel at all like eating his usual panino at his usual watering hole. He changed direction and made his way along Dundas Street towards the Art Gallery.

Stretching out before him all the way to where the Art Gallery of Ontario stood, the hustle and bustle of Chinatown was in full swing, the scent of the market was in the air. The original small Chinese shops awash in colourful crockery, statuettes of Bruce Lee and fat emperors with tiny genitalia, shared the street with the latest shops serving tourists, dumped here by tourist buses at the nearby station. Here they could buy t-shirts emblazoned with the red maple leaf and quartz wristwatches with a bobble head of Mickey Mouse. How paradoxical, thought Michele, that Chinatown, the mysterious and unfathomable Chinese city-within-the-city, was next door to the Art Gallery rising from the street as a bulwark of Western culture. About a hundred years ago Canada had imposed a head tax, a kind of entry fee, on immigrants from China. In 1904 the head tax had been fixed at $500. Chinese immigrants had been hired to work on the railroad, where they had toiled like beasts of burden, often dying on the job from hard labour and exertion. These days bilingual signs in Chinese and English towered over the buildings housing financial institutions; Western tourists passing by looked upon them with puzzlement, sighing with relief on seeing the English translation of the ideograms whose accuracy remained a mystery.

***

"Look, Michele, look! Albanians, Russians, Nigerians, Moroccans, Gypsies, and Slavs: we can't take it anymore. Italy has become the cesspool of the world, the ass..."

It had been last autumn, only a year ago, yet so far in the past. Raul had been driving in the rain in front of the central railway station in Milan when, on the corner of Via Fabio Filzi and Via Tonale, he violently forced the car window shut to avoid a beggar at the traffic light. Crouching in the passenger seat, Michele had focused on the *guardia di finanza* building on the right, with its marble bas-relief of yet another muscular nude turning grey in the smog. He was still baffled, after all these years, by Raul's aggressive nature. Merely sharing his intentions with him triggered his anger. It was impossible to talk ...

***

Down by Lake Ontario, at the end of Spadina Avenue, which snaked through the city like a dried-up riverbed, a baseball stadium capped by a dome had been built; the many carved grotesques of monkeys dangling from the outside walls gave it the appearance of a temple to the monkey gods, but in the sculptor's intention they symbolized the passionate support of the fans. In a nearby corner, next to the railway, stood a monument dedicated to recognizing the suffering of Chinese workers. Michele thought back to the Milano Centrale railway station in Milan where Albanians and droves of Africans lit up the darkness like ancient bas-reliefs in a city that went into hiding in its fogged-up homes.

***

"You just can't understand, Michele, you've lost touch with reality ... we've had it with ideas from twenty years ago – we must protect ourselves, protect our families... you've lost your marbles," Raul shouted at him, letting him out of the car onto Via Grazzo, leaving him alone in the midst of a gaggle of gigantic blonde prostitutes.

***

On Dundas Street, just before the Art Gallery, Michele looked up at the latest steel and glass condominium recently built by one of the many developers of Italian origin. The company name, Grotti, stood out on the billboards placed around the worksite. The head of the company was a developer who had received some bad press a few years earlier on account of shady connections with the political world. A scandal involving kickbacks and briberies had followed but quickly vanished from the press and from public memory.

On this particular day Michele had suffered one of his typical moments of discomfort, so he set out for the Art Gallery because the paintings and silence had a calming effect on him, distracting him from his worries. A Flemish painting, for example, with its universal market scenes of stifling and chaotic humanity, helped him forget his workplace, his co-workers and the expectorating street beggars by inspiring him to play a game of his own invention, a sort of treasure hunt for details. The grotesque vulgar dance in *The Peasant Wedding* by Pieter Brueghel the Younger: the red faces of the players and the farmers, the bride greedily counting the money she had been gifted for the occasion, and all the characters popping in and out in the painting, fascinated him to such a degree that his ninety-minute lunch break went by in a flash. And as Michele walked on, memories from the distant past washed up onto the shores of the present without his being aware of it.

***

Raul and Beppe running ahead of him and Tino towards the Rimac Stadium in Lima – it was the feast day of *Senor de los Milagros* – and Michele and Tino following behind, trying not to lose track of them among the thousands of people ... and the homegrown bullfighter who failed to kill his bull ... and another one heaved up into the infinite sky only to fall with a thud on the sand. But for Lucio it was a different spectacle ... his bull, tired of the painful game of hide-and-seek, of his many insults, was sobbing blood ... *uno, dos, tres* ... *Olè!* ... and the expectorating tramp shouting at him ... and Raul yelling at him and dumping him on the street ... and Beppe falling into the mud and crying out. There they stand idle in the drenching rain while Beppe begs for help ... and there is the bull stunned by Lucio's strike, standing briefly in a daze before crouching in agony, his shins kneeling on the sand now turning red with his blood, before a man delivers the *coup de grâce* by sinking a long blade into the scruff of his neck.

***

The sky in front of the Art Gallery was a swarming jungle of criss-crossing hydroelectric wires hanging from the poles, and Henry Moore's *Large Two Forms* on the corner of Dundas Street and John Street looked like a leftover, out-of-fashion brown thing, dumped in a hurry by tenants who had vacated the premises. Michele was overcome by a familiar sense of crushing oppression he often felt on this corner, made worse today by the heat and the encounter with the tramp.

As he negotiated the large, muffled entrance to the Gallery, his curiosity was piqued by a metallic installation. A small upside-down pine tree had been attached to an oil derrick's sharp pointed stem. Pressing a switch at the base of the structure set the pine tree in motion, and it descended slowly to sink into a demijohn filled with wine. The installation welcomed visitors to an exhibition called *Strangers in the Arctic: Ultima Thule and Modernity*. Michele decided to skip the Flemish painters; he paid for his ticket and walked briskly towards the exhibit, trying not to look at the paintings he knew very well, and apologizing to Giacometti for not stopping to pay homage to his adorable small sculpture, though he realized that he did not know Giacometti well enough to judge whether he would approve of the adjective adorable. He marched straight up to the second floor to look at the only Rothko painting in the Gallery's collection.

No. 1, White & Red.
He stood still in front of it, and for the first time after many days, months and years of observation and homage, he felt he finally understood the artist's intentions. That painting, according to the notes in the catalogue, marked the beginning of Rothko's darkest period. There's Beppe, bubbling up like a black bruise from the red rectangle framed by a fragile white barricade, a passionate cry rising from that sea of red; the impulse to tell the truth, unstoppable and uncontrollable, before the coming of darkness, of silence, of forgetfulness would bury it in the stillness of surrender, drown it in the thick, black high tide.

The time had come to tell the truth, not because of remorse, as many would think, but for a darker purpose, the sense of justice. Perhaps even for Beppe ... he must talk again ...

He moved away from *No. 1, White & Red*. Slowly he made his way to the entrance of *Ultima Thule*.

He was enchanted by the photographs of hooded fishermen pictured in front of their shacks surrounded by mud in the small fishing port, and the cemetery on the barren hill overlooking the bay with its frigid waters.

Michele had a mysterious attraction to the sun, the heat and the sea, and for this reason he had preferred South America and Africa, but since his fortieth birthday his tastes had changed. Now he was increasingly fascinated by places where the snow and the cold, silence and isolation reigned supremely. His nighttime dreams, visions of peace, found expression in a cavern that he reached only after an exhausting crossing over snow, and where he lay himself down, eyes closed, succumbing to a universal sleep, lulled by the slow rhythm of drops falling from the stalactites onto the ground, echoing like the slow muted drumming in a galley.

Between Rothko and 3 Windows

A feeling of euphoria and relaxation came bursting over him when, returning home from work, he would shut the door on the snowstorm, stretch out on the sofa in Valery's embrace and gaze at the swirl of snowflakes buffeted by the wind.

Together they dreamed of the deep, dark silence of Canadian forests. He had met Valeria, had learned English, and Canada had become his homeland. Canada was an infinite country, in spite of today's heat, in spite of his job in the office, in spite of the tramp who spat on him. Today, the squalor of the photos that captured a faraway yet familiar panorama of fishing shacks, of snow melting into mud, had a particular fascination for him, something he recognized, a summoning to push himself further out, to enter the great cavern that was the mystery of Canada, to leave sweltering Toronto behind.

Michele continued his visit of the Gallery's rooms, whose vaults echoed with the footfalls of a few visitors, dull as the sound of a billiard ball hitting the edge. From time to time the echo of a human voice in the empty, desolate rooms brought him back to reality. The exhibition had been installed in an especially dark corner of the Gallery, so dark that to gain access he had to grope his way towards it. The first screening showed a team of researchers going about their routine, the frightening sameness of days spent crossing the uncharted strip of a Norwegian forest. Michele watched a few images, got bored and moved on to the next room.

He noticed a header on the wall: *Henningsvaer, Norway, 68th parallel north. Three panoramic windows of a wooden, nondescript house are filmed close up from the outside between twelve and one o'clock at night. Inside is a party.* (A.K. Dolven.)

Feeling his way in the dark, Michele crossed a narrow corridor, reached the screening room and sat down on a couch facing the screen. A fixed frame camera was rigidly focused on the three windows beyond which no sign of life was visible, save for the occasional fluttering of the sheer curtains, brought on, Michele thought, by someone wishing to look outside.

For the most part the image never changed; always the three windows with the same party music spilling outside, and from time to time the screeching of a seagull. The typical light of a grey winter night lit up the surroundings. Gazing at the windows, Michele remembered the tramp who had spat on him while all around him the party music coming from the house was relentless, obsessive. How plebeian, Michele thought, just like his life in the government institution where hundreds of stockpiled faxes requested lists of companies producing extruders, transducers, gear shifters, pumps, submerged pumps, for liquids, for water, electric pumps ...

The Canada in which he lived was certainly different from the Great Lakes, different from the explorations in his dreams. Toronto was not Canada; it was a Swiss city in North America, polite and tolerant, where tramps could freely spit on pedestrians who did not give alms. That was an American scene, not Canadian; *A Mean Street* in keeping with Hollywood film culture that did not do justice to the land – a land of silences.

But then, what was this silence of which he dreamed? Gazing on that house with its pitiless, cool light, its music that could just as easily be heard in any parallel or meridian, the three silent and oblivious windows, one could only think of some new instrument of torture, a machine devised in a penal colony where the condemned died in the throes of an inevitable orgasm. The screeching of the seagull brought back to his mind all the tormented depressions of writers and directors from "the North," quickly disposed of with that handy label "Nordic." Just as Canada was dismissed with the label "the land of forests and lakes;" and Italy as the land of "spaghetti, sun, and corruption."

He sensed a presence behind him, but he could not see the face. He felt a sudden, unbearable pain in the scruff of his neck. It took only a moment, but Michele was dead. His body slid along the wall, gave a slight bucking, a muscle twitching, and became stiff.

He tried to rest his chin on his chest, but his head fell slowly outwards, like that of someone resisting sleep but finally giving in. That's how a Gallery security guard found him around two o'clock in the afternoon of June 5.

The guard ran off to get help, someone turned off the projector and the lights were turned on in that dark corner of the Gallery.

Chapter 2

As usual, Giovanni stormed into the office without knocking, ignored the files that cluttered the desk and placed his espresso coffee cup on some pictures of the president of Italy that were waiting to be published.

"*Zucchero?*" Giovanni asked, flashing the most maternal smile in his repertoire.

Luigi Sasta made no reply.

"*Zucchero?*" Giovanni insisted.

Finally Luigi fixed his gaze on Giovanni's meek eyes, noticed the halo left by the espresso cup's saucer on the picture of the Italian president, who was standing in an open roadster waving at the crowd, and patiently, not bothering to reply, moved the cup to an empty corner of the desk, a corner that Giovanni had not seen or had not bothered to see.

"*Dottori, u'café uidáut sciúgar is nott café,*" volunteered Giovanni, poet and former labourer, mustering all his seafaring ways with language.

"Thank you, Giovanni, but I like my coffee bitter," said Sasta, on the verge of losing his patience, hoping to avoid becoming angry and entering into an interminable diatribe that, day in, day out, lunch break after lunch break, had been going on for years and showed no signs of ever ending. The argument was always the same with Giovanni doggedly persisting in convincing him to put *sciúgar* in his coffee.

Luigi had been back in the newsroom only for a couple of days, after a two-week leave at home to recover from his angina attack. Nothing had changed at *Stampa Italica*, apart from an increase in the number of typos in the past few copies of the paper, including a glaring one in the heading of a column about the Toronto visit of a bishop who had come to build on the pastoral work started by his predecessors in Calabrian communities abroad. With a gleam in his eyes, Giovanni approached the desk again and, fronting a magician's touch, pulled a sugar bag out of thin air.

Luigi gave him a puzzled look, waiting for the old barista of the *Stampa Italica* bar, who made office deliveries of coffee only to him, to leave. He rummaged through the mess of papers and pictures on the desk for his packet of du Mauriers and lit up.

"*Dottori, de sigarett iz no gud for iu!*"

"Thanks, Giovanni." But you are the reason I am smoking. You make me so nervous!

Giovanni looked at him gravely, shaking his head in disapproval, and left the office only after he placed a sugar bag on the desk, which would end up like thousands before it, in the trash can. Nothing had changed at the paper, not Giovanni, not the never-ending line of postulants. Just a while ago in his office Luigi had seen a young man looking for work, the last for that day, but the story never changed: young people "wanting to move to Canada, to leave Italy because it was rotten to the core and offered no possibility of making it for anyone willing to work hard, but without connections." Luigi dropped his head; his brain still ached from the avalanche of knowledge, enthusiasm and ambition the young man had dumped on him. His hand still felt the powerful grip of his handshake. Looking about him he saw, as he did every day, the front page of the very first edition of *Stampa Italica* elegantly framed and hanging on the wall. Looking much younger, of course, he and the publisher were featured in a picture holding, triumphantly, the first edition of the paper. Almost daily, some Italian young man, hungry for work, appeared in his office, and every time he listened to these same complaints about Italy where "only those with connections could find employment."The sameness led him to think that in many cases it was an excuse. And they all sought refuge in his office after their first let-downs: some distant relatives in another country had not kept their promises, the many refusals by immigration offices, the few days of poorly paid, illegal work as bus boys or dishwashers in some hybrid Italian restaurant.

Maybe they all suddenly remembered an Italian community abroad and, ironically, many landed here in the belief that they would find an Italianized America. Luigi could not bring himself to dismiss them in a hurry, so he welcomed them into his office. From way back in 1954, the front page of the daily hanging in front of him spurred him to instill in them the willpower to struggle on, to have faith, to hope. He did not remember when he himself had lost this willpower, maybe as soon as a few front pages after the famous one hanging on the wall. Or maybe far back in 1991 … so he gathered his energies and launched into his well-rehearsed speech … which went something like this …

"In the 1950s, Italians arrived here in the thousands, the hundreds of thousands. Few of them could read and write, most spoke only their dialect, only a few spoke Italian … never mind English! Once unloaded at the harbour in Halifax, they went on to Montréal, to Toronto, to Ottawa; many went North, taking work in the forests as lumberjacks, or in the mines or railroads. It was hard being far away from home, without even receiving mail or news from Italy. Add to that the problem with language … jobs were available in manufacturing in the factories, and there was a need for craftsmen, storekeepers, but mostly labourers. Have you had a look at Toronto? Well, in those years it was little more than a village. Then in just a few years we saw the rise of skyscrapers, buildings, homes, and do you know who was behind all this? Italians and other desperate workers like them who landed here from all parts of the world. Ten, twelve hours and more per day, day in, day out, working like donkeys only to go home to put up new brick walls, tear down old ones to build a dream home for their children, to tend to a miserable vegetable garden that they called *bechiarda*, from the Englsh word "backyard." Even today, when so many are economically well-off and have no need to grow tomatoes and vegetables in such tiny spaces, they still do it, so they don't forget their beginnings. By the way ... do you smoke? ... No? Good for you! There are only a few of us left who smoke. The few of us here and those who live in Québec!

"Back then we were a small, privileged group of Italians because we had been to school, and once we immigrated to Canada with our families we tried to teach the basics of English, and of Italian, to our fellow countrymen and women. When we launched this paper it was like an explosion of collective joy; we sold papers by the thousands ... at bus stations ... on construction sites ... everywhere you looked you could pick up a copy of *Stampa Italica*.

"It was a golden age for us, and for many years we were the only press service, we had a 'direct line,'" (Luigi hated this phrase), "to the Italian community, which was grateful to us because we explained Canada in simple words. But today," Luigi sighed, "we are in the second, third and, in many cases, fourth generation; children and grandchildren no longer speak Italian, they are ashamed of fathers who stammer along in dialect, who can only babble a few words of English, making them look bad, while we publish a newspaper that sells only a few wretched copies to seniors who are alienated from their children and ..."

"But I see people waiting eagerly for the start of the World Cup, and it seems to me that there is still some pride ..." the day's visitor chirped in, unwilling to surrender and accept Luigi's desolate scenario.

"Don't get me started on that," Luigi Sasta jumped in, implying that it was just a crock of shit, that when you really looked into it, all this flag-waving pride was just the symptom of a malaise, an inability to integrate. But he did not want to depress the young man in front of him – as he had done with all the previous ones who had sat in his chair telling him their stories of how everyone was capable and honest, but unlucky – so he asked him for his address and phone number.

"I'll see what I can do," and the slip of paper ended up with all the others, in the drawer full of resumes and telephone numbers. The interview, such as it was, came to an end. Luigi sipped his coffee, gazed beyond the window, and thought back to his long, despairing monologue, which had remained the same and which he repeated verbatim every single time. Long rows of townhouses stretched out before him in a panorama of villas and monster homes fronted by large, shining porticos and huge white pillars. Flapping in the wind, Italian and Canadian flags looked down from balconies and rooftops on houses surrounded by massive walls, jealously guarding the new-found wealth from unwanted outside corruption.

He had seen the rich people's ghetto, as someone had labelled it, of the fabulous 1970s and 80s. He had watched that bottom feeder spread its tentacles from Toronto's downtown towards the suburbs, gobbling up farmland on the way till it grew into a new creature: a new downtown spreading its tentacles into never-ending farmland that offered no obstacles to the ambition of developers, whose fortunes had grown rapidly and miraculously thanks to an angst for exodus that had gripped Italians, eager to leave the historic centre of the city, as if seeking safety from the plague, as though ashamed of their past, in order to set roots in these vast neighbourhoods of wealth, the new enclave of *italianità* in the infinite and anorexic Po valley that is Ontario.

Luigi did not write these things in his *Stampa Italica*, the readers would take offence: how could he blame a community that for decades had sweated blood to create a better life than had been possible in Italy? There was some truth in this, Luigi thought: Italians, and not just them, Portuguese, Chinese, Ukranians, Jamaicans, Indians – all those millions of wretched people who had escaped and were still escaping, fleeing from their homelands to finally wash up on these shores, to defend themselves from their own people, the system, from everything and everyone. So many parallel stories of humanity landing here, in pursuit of what? To do what? To work and reproduce only to lock themselves up in marble cathedrals with hardwood floors.

His newspaper followed on the heels of this exodus, moving away from the centre towards the first, second and third suburbs, beyond the surrounding walls, far away from the downtown, pushing beyond into the countryside where a few scrawny trees marked a new frontier to be conquered, built up with other monster homes in a style that aped the White House, a *"nio-uoscingtón"* style capped by Italian and Canadian flags. Luigi asked himself if this was any different than what was going on in Rome, in New York. Do people not move away in search of green space? Even here there was a rejection of the city, of urban life. Could it be due to an anarchist rejection of a life centrally controlled by the temples of commerce?

There were no bedroom communities anymore, commuter towns where practitioners of the arts and crafts could collapse from exhaustion after the daily toil downtown. They had been replaced by the colonial enclaves of small and great landowners who had come together into an illusory Alamo, arrogant as the historic one. There had been flood, but this Noah's Ark, with its marble bridge and golden holds, shut its door to all other ethnic couples not belonging to the bloodline of the captain and his consort.

"Before this, what had this Italian-Canadian been?" Luigi Sasta asked himself. He could only think of the famous joke about the zebra's stripes: a white horse with black stripes, or a black horse with white stripes? Who was an Italian-Canadian today?

These thoughts buzzed around in his head like swarms of irritating insects. Just yesterday the publisher had called a meeting ostensibily to discuss new cuts, but in reality to announce that he would be unable to pay their salaries this month, and possibly next month as well, adding that any desertion would be perfectly justifiable. As the editor of the paper, Luigi sat next to him, looking at the staff, his face ashen.

But he felt a tightening in his heart when he thought that it had come down to this: sharing the last remaining munitions among the frontline soldiers before the final battle. He was well aware of the dilemma, knew that his staff had no other option but to work here in the vain hope of some new miserable funding. Many were too old, some were insufficiently qualified, and the rest spoke little, heavily accented English, and they could not write it very well. But above all, none of them would admit that *Stampa Italica* was the only place where they could practice their favourite activity, journalism; patch writing, to be sure, but journalism nonetheless. And so everyone lined up to join the resistance, taking up arms in that barren no man's land. The publisher was satisfied, but Luigi felt sick. He focused on the movement of traffic along the highway, with cars speeding towards the exit, then grasped the door handle and rushed out towards the newsroom.

Sitting around a TV that had been placed on the desks, designers and reporters were following World Cup commentaries and forecasts. Save for the sound of cigarette puffs here and there, or a sigh, the silence was deafening. Luigi asked himself where he might have found the energy, not to speak of the motivation, to dash off into the newsroom when his small team of reporters was lounging in front of the TV. Only *Signorina* Arianna, the deputy editor, pushing sixty or thirty or a hundred and ten, was busily cutting away pieces from the ANSA news agency to be sorted, printed and passed on to the "Italia" desk, Arazzi's desk, to be clear, but he was deeply focused on the TV broadcast. Other pieces from the agency would end up stacked on the pile on the "Foreign Affairs" desk, but with a decidedly Italian editorial line under the guidance of Snervato, who was also deeply engaged in the sports broadcast.

"What's the verdict?" Luigi directed his question, wearily, to that walrus, Mogli, the gout-ridden sports reporter forever glued to the TV, who thought nothing of interviewing his relatives for comments on the game for the day's sports event, and who was known in the newsroom as the "hermit crab" because he never left his wheelchair and kept the TV playing on the shelf directly above his head. There was no answer, so he repeated his question, and Arazzi, who thought of himself as a commentator because he edited the "Italia" page by simply adding to the comments borrowed from Canadian papers, answered that according to many, Italy ranked among the teams favoured to win.

"Should I go to the Italian community and pick up some comments?" Arazzi asked, smiling enthusiastically, flashing his nicotine-blackened teeth.

Luigi looked at him, long and hard. "Arazzi, what do you expect Italians to tell you? That they are unhappy? Just make up some comments and send a photographer to Little Italy for a group photo … and you, Mogli, why don't you call your friends at Bar Italia, see what the mood is like and write a report on it …"

"I'm on it," Mogli replied, glued to his chair, without turning his head.

"By the way, chief, Sergeant Stevens called," added Arazzi.

"What did he want?"

"I don't know, but he said to call as soon as possible …"

"When did he call?"

"Half an hour ago, maybe an hour ..."

"And you tell me now?"

In spite of his 35 years, Arazzi looked back at him like a smirking, spoiled brat caught with his hands in the cookie jar. He lit a cigarette and returned his gaze to the TV, emitting a loud puff as if to say that when the national team is playing, everything is permitted.

"Give me his number," Luigi said.

"*Signorina* Arianna has it," answered Arazzi without bothering to face him.

"Oh sure, the poor *Signorina* Arianna has it ..." Luigi realized that Arazzi had stopped listening to him.

Signorina Arianna, with the shy little face of an agency mouse, got up from her desk, showing her Svetlana Stalin summer dress, in blue linen with dark buttons and a white collar; foraged among the pile of papers; squealed in joy as though she'd been given a raise, or more to the point, been paid her current wages; singled out a piece of paper and brought it over, beaming, to Luigi. He took it without thanking her. The *Signorina* made a face, and Luigi was quick to inquire about her health.

"I'm better, thank you, *Dottore*, better ... it's nothing serious really, just some rheumatisms ... though I shouldn't take them lightly with all this humidity. And you ... how are you?"

Luigi, smothered by the radiant approach of the blue dress and the mothball fragrance of *Signorina* Arianna's breath, made his retreat, thanked her and turned away. He heard the *Signorina* complain about the smoke, aware that his reminder that the city had banned smoking in public places and in offices had fallen on deaf ears. Luigi thought that *Signorina* Arianna must be the only person left in the newsroom who had not realized that they were about to close shop, and he regretted his rudeness.

In the newsroom and the offices, the heat was stifling, with no air coming in through the open windows. *Stampa Italica* was in arrears with the rent, and the landlord had cut off the air conditioning.

Luigi glanced at the horrendous clock on the wall: the face showed a soccer player from the national team with splayed legs serving as hands to mark the time. It was almost three o'clock. No news had come in till now, but *Stampa Italica* was sure to lead with the World Cup. They were in the clear for the next few days. He lit another cigarette, picked up the receiver and dialed Sergeant Stevens' number.

"It's Sasta, Luigi Sasta, from *Stampa Italica* ..."

"Luigi, how are you? It's been a long time, eh?" Sergeant Stevens mumbled without giving Luigi any time to respond.

"I called you because something really interesting has happened: a murder, not the usual run-of-the-mill, but a really strange one ... Does the name Michael Karrier ring a bell? ... In his forties, very elegant, medium build, dark eyes, short, curly hair, beard, Italian for sure ... you know ... whenever there's a murder it's Italians or Jamaicans."

Luigi glowered at the Sergeant's remarks, thinking that, in spite of all the time they had known each other, nothing had really changed: the same son-of-a-bitch racist cop. Like taxi drivers ... like truck drivers ... sons of bitches, mostly.

"Where?"

"At the Art Gallery of Ontario, but come on over and I'll fill you in."

"Did you say murder ...?"

"What would you make of a hole in the poor guy's neck ... would you call it suicide? In Italy, would you *wops* get away with calling this a suicide?"

"Mafia?"

"I'm not sure, don't know, the victim seems ..."

"Seems ...?"

"Can't tell ... unusual ..."

In the past Luigi had worked with Sergeant Stevens on many cases. An accidental friendship had been born during their collaboration on the case of a Mafia boss shot dead on his way home, but over the years it had grown stronger as they had worked together on many cases, mostly involving Italians as victims or murderers. Luigi had always had a soft spot for crime news, for homicides. It was a strange obsession for which he found no explanation.

They had worked together in this way until that fateful day in 1991 when, in response to citizen protests, an investigation on some developers intent on building in a public park led to the discovery of a large ring of corrupt dealings involving many politicians, some of them with Italian last names. That had been the last shining moment for *Stampa Italica*, as it had scooped every other daily, naming names and pointing fingers against some big shots in local governments. Soon after, like a volcano that stops rumbling, the whole thing had just vanished; Stevens had risked his job and had been threatened with a promotion and transfer to some Sardinia in northern Ontario, while Luigi had been crucified by the leaders of his own community. They had agreed to meet late one night at the Mars Diner, on the corner of College and Bathurst Streets, and after some lengthy muttering in front of a couple of bowls of cooked fruit, they had decided to pull the plug, not so much out of fear, but because they had realized that they had reached their end point.

"Sasta, there are just too many of them ... mayors, would-be mayors, councillors, builders, the usual heavy hitters ... they'll burn us ..."

Stevens had twirled his spoon in the fruit bowl.

"I've been labelled a traitor to the community ... apparently dirty linen is a family affair." They forget we are in Canada now ...

Luigi had kept this last thought to himself. He did not wish to give Stevens any satisfaction.

That was about all they had said to each other that night. They had finished the cooked fruit and quickly said their goodbyes without shaking hands. They had lost touch, save for a token Christmas greeting and, from time to time, hearing some mentions from common friends. So many years have gone by, Luigi thought, maybe we were just cowards, and he made a wide sweep with his arm, as if to clear away his melancholy thoughts.

This murder could command some real attention; it had been a long time since such a strange homicide had occurred, apart from the usual settling of scores between Mafia families and predictable reprisals between rival bike gangs.

"The Gallery is an odd place," suggested Luigi.

"Certainly unusual for the mafia," added Stevens.

"Why? Can't the Mafia kill in a gallery? ... What about the murder weapon?" Luigi asked, in his most brooding manner.

"A knife, possibly a short blade, I am waiting for confirmation from forensics ..."

"Where is it?" Luigi asked, waking up from his reverie.

"The killer took it with him," Sergeant Stevens replied.

"OK. I'll send someone over."

"Good, see you there!" Stevens said, certain that Luigi would not assign another journalist to this case. But just as Luigi was thinking he might send a reporter, a loud scream rose from the newsroom, a collective crying out.

"What happened?" Sergeant Stevens asked. "Did you slash someone's throat?"

Luigi did not respond and put the receiver down with a sneer. Sergeant Stevens was not an evil man, but he did have a quirky sense of humour, not to mention the code of ethics of a racist son of a bitch. Luigi slipped on his jacket. Everyone was glued to the TV just now, and sending someone else might result in a mutiny at *Stampa Italica*. And in any case, it would give him an opportunity to visit his daughter Elena, who lived near the Gallery.

No sooner had he stepped into the editing room than *Signorina* Arianna jumped at him, but Luigi put a rude end to her complaining even before she could begin.

"*Signorina*, leave me a column on the front page with space for a picture. I don't think I will be back, I'll dictate the piece!"

"Very well, *Direttore* Sasta!"

"And *Signorina*, call Tony, the photographer, and tell him to join me at the Art Gallery. After that he can go to Little Italy to take some shots of soccer fans. I'll be sure to remind him, but now I want him there pronto!"

"OK, boss, *arrivederci*," *Signorina* Arianna said, bowing her head.

"*Arrivederci*, I'll see you tomorrow," Luigi said, in a loud voice.

No one bothered to take notice that the editor-in-chief of *Stampa Italica* was leaving.

Chapter 3

As he left the newspaper offices to get into his 1981 Subaru, the bright sun blinded Luigi. The delivery truck pulled into the parking lot with the returns from the previous week, when Luigi had been forced to take mandatory leave because of his angina. Working from home, he had followed up on the news of a statistical report from the school board pointing out that a large number of students failed to finish high school, with a series of editorials on the difficulties faced by young people of Italian origin as they tried to integrate into the larger society. Once again he had been accused of not rising up to the defence of his own people. Community leaders and members of Parliament of Italian origin mounted a letter-writing campaign against the newspaper: whenever he was critical of the Italian community (there were no sacred cows for him!) the paper's readership seemed to grow by the thousands. In response to these letters, Luigi had written, in one go, a piece focusing on the very first wave of immigration at the end of the 19th century when, along with many honest people, some criminals had also landed here, in the first Italian settlements in the downtown area (not far from the Art Gallery), creating a protection racket aimed at Italian immigrants, giving rise to the first cell of an organization that would end up as the Mafia. He ended the piece by stating that these shady characters did not represent the community, that we must remain ever vigilant to overcome prejudice. It was not by sweeping these facts under the rug that we could build a new life; turning a blind eye would not make us better, Luigi concluded. Turning a blind eye, he glossed, amounted to turning away from the struggles, the back-breaking work, the economic conditions of privilege that led to isolation, the exploitation of new immigrants on construction sites run by Italian developers, the prejudice heaped on them. It's possible that Luigi had been writing more for himself than for his readers. Yesterday, as he had done each time Luigi wrote a piece on the community, the publisher had stormed into his office, thumping the newspaper on the desk.

Luigi and the publisher had grown old together since those days in 1954 when they had gone about distributing the newspaper in construction sites and on the streets. Luigi thought back to Italians storming the first *Stampa Italica* van to buy up copies fresh from the printing press. He watched them, the newspaper rolled under their arms, or held tightly in their hands, as they returned to work to the pneumatic drills, the assembly lines, saw them navigating waves of cement laying down a sidewalk, saw them sink into the sewers, climb scaffolding. As often happens when you get old, the past took on a heroic hue.

The publisher was old and puffing; the few strands of hair left on his head looked unnatural, frequently glued to his scalp by embarrassing rivulets of sweat brought on by the oppressive, stifling heat. And Luigi had his angina. Forty years together and their arguments had remained unchanged; they fought as they always did, still disliked each other, and had never made an effort to pretend to even care for one another. But they stuck together: Siamese twins, glued to each other by the memories of all those years gone by.

"Here we go again, Sasta!" The publisher had started in on him, as he had done many times before, with a nod to those fateful days of 1991. "I have just finished talking on the phone to a dozen or so really pissed off people …"

"Look on the bright side. At least we've picked up a few more readers!" Luigi had blurted out bluntly.

Between Rothko and 3 Windows

They had stared at each other intensely in the face, like animals poised to pounce, but before a fight could ensue the publisher had turned away and left.

Luigi had been blinded by the sun's reflection off the window of a bus. He lit up a du Maurier, opened up his car door, lazily threw his jacket onto the passenger seat next to him, sat down and loosened his tie. Soon he would retire, this was the right time to leave work and write the book he'd been meaning to write on his community. Who would be interested in the tragedy of broken lives after the great crossing? Perhaps he should write a book for Italy, for those who were not even aware of all the Italians who had left it, who had been forced to leave; rightful descendants of a country of explorers and inventors; forced to drop the final syllable of their last names to avoid being mistaken for Italians in a country where Italians could not gather on the sidewalks in groups larger than three without risking a police beating. Maybe he should write a thriller ... maybe he should write nothing. Maybe he should return to Italy ... he was fed up with the long winters.

What a strange homicide, he thought; the victim had been stabbed in the back of his neck with a pointed weapon ... but who was this victim? Killed in an art gallery ... what was he up to in the Gallery? Was he there to meet his assassin? At first blush it looked like an out-of-the-ordinary killing ... something from the past ...

It took him almost half an hour to drive to College Street, but finally he was in Little Italy, his childhood haunts since immigrating here with his mother, both of them sponsored by his father, a craftsman from Sardinia, a very skilled wrought iron worker whose chiselled low railings still adorned the gardens of many houses in Little Italy.

Apart from some vague flashbacks of chases through the narrow streets and waiting at the wine cellar in Via Garibaldi, Luigi had few memories of his infancy in Cagliari. He would miss the sea forever, but he remembered little else. He had just turned six when he had landed in Canada, and soon he had been absorbed into a new school and a new group of friends. In the beginning his family had lived in a house with a dozen other people on the corner of College and Clinton Streets. Like thousands of other Italians, they had ended up living in Little Italy, and as soon as things improved, his father had bought a house on Mansfield Avenue, close to St Francis's church where, even to this day, mass was celebrated in Italian for a congregation of a few dozen older people and the occasional obligatory appearance of newly elected Italian politicos. During the Easter celebrations thousands upon thousands of Italians gathered on the streets to take in the fully costumed procession re-enacting the flagellation of Christ at the hands of centurions. They flocked here from all parts of Toronto. Luigi was always embarrassed by it, thinking that Canadians came to the procession with the same attitude one takes to the zoo. Television cameras focused their colonial eyes on the anguished face of the Christ, and on hundreds of older peasants, all dressed up in their Sunday best to take part in an ancient country fair.

Mansfield Avenue was a quiet little street, with low-rise houses fronted by Italian gardens. Luigi was acquainted with everyone who lived there, and the few square metres of manicured greenery reminded him of the sense of decorum of the Italians and Portuguese who lived on Mansfield. In winter, the gardens and the sidewalks on which they bordered were always free of snow, in spite of the pile-ups that had been left on the corners by the City. Once, in a College Street bar, Luigi had been engaged in conversation with an Italian, possibly from Milan, who had explained to him that this sense of order and cleanliness was a relic of the past, a memory of an Italy that was no longer. On the coldest days, Luigi had observed this Italian dress up in unlikely overcoats and cloaks topped by misshapen Sicilian caps, yet in springtime he had been the first one to be seen on his bicycle. Even before he had uttered a word, Luigi had taken him as someone newly arrived from Italy. It must have been the way he wore his ties (large Windsor knot, muted tones) or his way of checking his appearance, reflected in a shop or car window, to make sure that all was as it should be.

"You see," the Italian had said to him, sipping his oversweetened coffee, "back home we do not do these things. We do not leave the house in the morning to shovel away the snow, we do not have such little houses, and most of us live in condominiums. And, personally, I do not like manual labour," he had finished up, taking himself very seriously.

"But as the City forces us to clear up those three or four metres of sidewalk, I have come to an agreement with my Portuguese neighbour. He clears the snow from his sidewalk and mine, and I just look on! No, it's not true that I just look on ... on winter mornings it's so nice to lounge in bed for a few more minutes, listening to the scraping of my neighbours' shovels."

In summer, as he walked these narrow streets, Luigi thought he was in a residential area behind the hotels and *pensioni* of a seaside village. It pleased him to know that on the street in which he came to live, in a house from the 1920s, there had been a welcome centre for Irish immigrants. This continuity in history, the consistency of comings and goings, made him feel good. As the 1970s had come to an end, and the Italians, who had made their small fortunes, did not wish to live downtown any longer and started an exodus towards newly built suburbs, Luigi had married Mariuccia and settled in the Annex, a neighbourhood favoured by radical intellectual WASPs and visited by many political exiles. But when his wife had died, something had moved him to return to live in Little Italy.

Luigi loved waking up early in the morning so he could walk along that strip of College Street aflame in the crimson light of the rising sun. At this time the couriers delivered the morning papers, and Luigi would sneak into the bar where old Michele had left his broom on the wet pavement to take his place behind the espresso machine. In a slow procession, the place filled up with all the night-time buzzards: wasted youth after a wild night, old men who slept little, cops who had finished their rounds. They sipped their cappuccinos in silence, dutifully, something that, as Luigi never tired of pointing out, must be done only in the morning, not after dinner as many Canadians did. The church still insisted on kicking about its bells, in spite of many complaints from citizens who did not want their Sunday morning sleep interrupted by the bucolic tolling. Luigi was pleased to meet up with the few seniors who were still around, the other faces of Italian success: the faces of those who never made it, who stayed in Little Italy and did not run off to hide in neoclassic villas in the suburbs. Most of them were old and waited for Sunday visits from their children to spend the day together in aimless chatter over plates of homemade pasta.

That afternoon the Portuguese and Italian bars on College Street were overflowing with people. A hustle-bustle of patrons coming and going on the street, nibbling on a biscuit, lustily licking an ice cream, only to stop and loiter in small groups to argue, more than likely, over the looming World Cup games.

Luigi Sasta had now reached Kensington Market, the old Jewish market that had become a kind of Saint- Germain-des-Prés of the third world with its old run-down houses, home to Jamaican bohemians, bikers wasted like worn-out tire treads, drugged Indian-Africans, washed out punks who had survived the night, Somalis recently arrived after the civil war, and the Portuguese who still thronged the fish markets and fruit and vegetable stores. The stagnant heat hung over the market where Luigi Sasta had slipped in with his Subaru, to be in a familiar crowd after the empty anonymity of the suburbs. He skirted around the university, but the memories of the rigorously tended gardens, the neo-gothic buildings, the English-style campus made him feel uncomfortable, gave him the sense of not belonging, of exclusion. Elena, his daughter, taught film studies at this university, but since Mariuccia's death he and Elena had taken separate paths.

He would invite himself to dinner. No! Elena was not fond of surprises, his in particular. Better to call her and invite her out. No, even better to call her and ask if he could drop in just to say hello. He turned onto Beverly Street towards the Art Nouveau building housing the Italian Consulate and on which soared the tricolour flag, giving the building the look of an outpost built to control the border with Chinatown. Waiting for the traffic lights to change, Luigi studied the gait of a Chinese girl crossing the street; focused, quiet, mysterious, clutching a shopping bag while all around her the market echoed with the chirping of shoppers besieging the stands for fresh fruit and exotic produce.

It occurred to him that a true revolution was taking place in these neighbourhoods, on College Street, in Chinatown, in Kensington; it was here that the voice and the sounds of Asia were winning out over the climate, the education, the culture and the daily life of the founding people. It was here that the city was changing, taken over by new beating hearts and aggressive cell systems.

Dundas Street, on which the Art Gallery stood, was closed off to traffic. Luigi parked in the vicinity and made his way towards the first police blockade, only to be stopped by an officer. He mentioned that Sergeant Stevens, homicide squad, was waiting for him. A gigantic police officer made a call on his ham radio and, once he was given the OK, let Luigi through. The street in front of the Gallery thronged with curious bystanders. A police cordon kept them at some distance from the stairs leading to the Gallery's main entrance. There was confusion all around. Firefighters had blocked two streetcars at one end of the street; police cars, and television crews with their vans, made it all the worse. The crowd was polite, curious, but not involved, and it grew without creating a disturbance, apart from a few kids who had cut through the yellow ribbon cordon into the "off limits" area, and had climbed onto Henry Moore's sculpture, *Large Two Forms*, which looked like two very large, deflated doughnuts. Luigi thought that Moore himself would have taken some pleasure in knowing that he gave some refuge to the iconoclastic innocence of the children.

Luigi climbed the stairs into the Art Gallery with a new-found vigour and enthusiasm he could not explain. He was stopped once again, but when he mentioned his appointment with Sergeant Stevens, they let him through. On entering Weston Hall he saw the metallic tower with the upside-down pine tree. The installation was blocked; frozen, as in a snowstorm.

Making his way among the toing and froing of police officers, he moved quickly across the entrance hall, through the first exhibition rooms, and climbed the stairs until he saw the ribbon marking off the scene of the crime just in front of the entrance to the *Strangers in the Arctic: Ultima Thule and Modernity* exhibit.

He remembered having seen this exhibit only a few weeks ago, remembered the feelings of infinite sadness and his desire to escape; maybe to Italy, in the Marches area, maybe to the sea, to satisfy an urgent craving for cheerful Mediterranean truths, for a biblical return home after many failed attempts to integrate into another nation, going in vain against the grain, struggling uselessly with the rhetoric of the Italian who has made it, the Italian who takes refuge in his enclave of wealth …

From the start there had been a major misunderstanding between Canadians and newly landed Italians. For Canadian institutions there was only one Italy, the one represented by immigrants who had come looking for work. On the other hand, Italians were convinced that they could protect themselves against discrimination, ethnic prejudice, and the class structure by taking refuge in an Italian past they had not lived through and whose splendours were foreign to them. Luigi had tried to blend in with the Canadian crowd, but everyone took him for an Italian. Maybe the accent gave him away, or his appearance, or his work as an Italian journalist for an Italian language daily, which he saw as his major drawback.

Luigi could go on for hours discussing and reflecting on the question of the integration of Italians in Canada, but he had come to the Art Gallery for another reason, which immediately cleared his mind of any speculation.

He had a clear memory of the exhibit, especially of the room in which television monitors, set up beside large blackboards covered with writings, showed a set of bizarre tennis matches between the author of the installation and another unwary player. The deep silence of the room was broken only by the sharp blows of the rackets which, more often than not, flayed the balls, an effect that was far from amusing in its grotesque and almost chilling impact.

Luigi Sasta looked over between the two screening rooms and saw Sergeant Stevens approach him, arms wide open.

"*Come stai?* Do you see what you Italians are capable of?"

Luigi smiled uncomfortably, but in the end he caved and fell into his sincere embrace, while technicians from the forensics unit walked past them clutching their toolkits and briefcases as they left the scene of the crime. Time had stood still; Stevens's racist jokes were still the same. But he had aged, and his big Irish face was a criss-crossing of bluish veins brought on by too much drink, maybe, or exposure to the long Canadian winters.

"What are we guilty of now?" Luigi asked.

"Put these on before you make a racket," Stevens ordered, throwing him a pair of rubber gloves.

Before entering into the room Luigi had read the title of the screening and remembered clearly what it was about. He had sat down in front of the three windows for a few minutes, to speculate, but mostly to rest. The film was pretty sordid, not much different from the static, desolate spectacle of the dead body sitting, eyes wide open, abandoned on the love seat.

Luigi scrutinized the victim's face, moving his gaze along its rather strong features, which piqued his interest, even though they were twisted by rigor mortis, by surprise at the pain of the blow that had killed him. He walked around the body and made a note of the large, deep cut on the nape of the neck.

"What did you say his name was?" Luigi asked in a low voice.

"Michael Karrier, Italian, *Michele Carrieri*," Sergeant Stevens replied with a strong accent, mangling the identity of the victim.

"Never learned any Italian? Not even to make an effort at a decent pronunciation of a name or surname?" Luigi hissed, lighting a cigarette.

"Are you still smoking?" Sergeant Stevens was astonished.

"Always," Sasta replied.

"I heard you had some health problems …"

"Slander!"

"Ever see him?" asked Sergeant Stevens.

"No!" Luigi Sasta blurted out, asking himself why the dead guy decided to anglicize his name. This had gone out of fashion in Canada but had been common practice in the 50s and before when Italians tried to blend in because a last name ending in a vowel was a source of shame. The victim wore an elegant grey suit, his tie loosened.

"Who was he? What did he do?" Luigi asked, his gaze fixed on the body.

"He worked nearby in an office belonging to your government," replied Sergeant Stevens.

"Which government? The Canadian? The Italian?" Luigi Sasta asked impatiently.

"The Italian one, of course ... the one you change every year ... he was a consultant or something in a commercial office," Sergeant Stevens said with a smile, almost happy to have irritated Luigi, a game he had mastered many years ago.

"Found anything? Have you questioned the security people? The Gallery staff? *Dai su, in fretta*, Stevens! Give me all the details of the case; don't keep the best for yourself like you always do."

"... Michael Carrieri – did I pronounce it correctly this time? – forty-three years old, came to Canada in 1985. Still not clear on what he did before or where he came from. We're still investigating, don't know very much other than he lived with a professor from York University, Valeria Furlon ... normal life, unassuming, the co-workers we've been able to trace don't know much more, no significant friendships, as far as we know up to now –"

"Where is his wife?" asked Luigi, loitering about the body.

"There is no wife ... isn't it strange for an Italian man not to be married, Luigi?"

"Do you give a shit, Stevens? You can't even see beyond your red Irish nose. It's like telling you that whisky is only English ..."

Sergeant Stevens flashed him a sly smirk. "We questioned the security guard who found the body, nothing interesting, we are checking up on all employees, staff and volunteers, I'll keep you posted ... any other questions?"

"Only about a hundred or so ... How was he killed? Did he carry a wallet? Any papers? Was he robbed? What was the murder weapon?"

"We should wait for the results of the autopsy, but my theory is that someone killed him with a sharp knife, a dagger in the nape of the neck. If you look closely, you'll notice that there's hardly any blood. This could mean that the heart stopped pumping due to sudden death –"

"After which the murderer pulled back his weapon, wiped it on the sleeve of the victim's suit …" Luigi took a deep puff of his du Maurier, pointing to a coagulated bloodstain on Carrieri's sleeve.

"We found the usual things in his wallet: credit cards, his staff ID to get into his office, membership cards, calling cards," Stevens said.

"What about forensics? What do they say?" Luigi asked, backing away from the body to take a good look from further off, to take in the scene of the crime.

"Yes! We have their report. The coroner fixed the time of death between one and two in the afternoon … the body was found around two thirty …"

"It mustn't be easy killing a man with a knife to the nape of the neck," mumbled Luigi as he approached the screen.

"What was that?"

"Nothing, I was musing out loud about the assassin's skills … It's not enough to strike a hard blow, you must know the right spot and the angle. Have you called his wife, his live-in partner?" Luigi stopped right in front of the screen.

"An officer is on his way to pick her up and bring her to the morgue for the identification of the body. I wasted some time before authorizing the removal of the body," he added, badgering him, "only to wait for you …"

"I'll go see if the photographer is here … back in a second," said Luigi as he left the room.

"OK, I'll have the body removed," replied Sergeant Stevens.

On reaching the exit, Luigi watched a group of policemen laughing riotously while a fellow policewoman fiddled with the on/off button of the installation just inside the Gallery's entrance. The upside-down pine tree dunked its crown into the wine and rose up again to its perch. Luigi saw Tony trying

Between Rothko and 3 Windows

to make his way, without much success, past the police cordon at the main door, and came to his rescue, telling the officers that he was the official photographer for *Stampa Italica*.

"Take as many pictures as you can, and if anyone tries to stop you, tell him Sergeant Stevens gave you the OK; should they stop you, leave the Gallery, take some shots of the curious crowd of onlookers … make sure to take some brochures of the exhibit with you … then go to Little Italy and take some shots of people there."

"Boss … *uano minut* … please?"

Tony Camarro, the photographer of *Stampa Italica*, had never learned English, or Italian for that matter. And like many Italians he had invented a language of his own.

"Not now, not now, go … it's on the second floor," Luigi said, fully aware that Tony wanted to talk about his paycheque. He patted him on the back and sent him on his way inside the Gallery.

"We'll talk tomorrow …"

Luigi Sasta made his way back into the Gallery, but this time he walked in towards the great hall with the Moore exhibition. The victim had changed his name, but why? Luigi mulled this over again and again as he walked among the models, silent and huge in the great hall echoing with his footsteps.

A Mafia killing … seems unlikely, but it is definitely the work of a professional killer … killing with a knife and with such precision … it's not for everybody … poor guy … he was looking at the screening … why the fascination with those three windows …?

Luigi took out his cellphone.

"*Signorina* Arianna, yes, it's me, Sasta … the headline for that piece for the front page should be *'ITALIANO UCCISO ALL'ART GALLERY'* and the sub-head *'omicidio in una sala del famoso museo di Toronto'* … OK? I'll call you in an hour or so with the piece …"

The publisher would be happy, not that Luigi cared all that much.

In the majestic silence, Moore's "draped reclining figure," her legs stretched out, her torso erect, focused her cornea-less eyes on the nearby/faraway, on nowhere in particular, her gaze dead and mysterious like Michele Carrieri's body.

Luigi took out his cellphone and dialed Elena's number.
"Elena?"
"Is it you, *Papà*?"
"Yes, it's me. What are you doing later on? Do you want to go out for dinner?" Luigi asked.
"No, but why don't you come here?"
"You'll cook?"
"Of course ... you have something to say about my cooking? If you don't wish to come ..."
"No, of course I'll come ..."
"Is something wrong? Are you feeling OK?"
"Yes, I'm feeling fine, and you?"
"I'll see you here at 6 tonight!"

Elena hung up, leaving Luigi with the impression that both he and his daughter thought of the telephone only as a tool to get their work done; they did not look to it for intimate communication, as something to be used by two people who had not spoken to each other as they might have wanted to, or should have, for far too long.

Luigi looked at the sculpture. Elena was not yet aware of his angina. He put the cellphone in his pocket and returned to the screening room. Michele Carrieri's cadaver had been placed in a black body bag and moved onto a gurney. The victim's face disappeared from view as the paramedics pulled on the long zipper, closing the bag. Luigi took off his gloves and let them fall onto a cardboard box, where they joined the pile left by the technical people from forensics and the other detectives. He lit a cigarette but was immediately approached by someone in a double-breasted suit with a horrible rainbow-coloured tie, a lackey with the museum or maybe with forensics, who reminded him that smoking was not allowed. Luigi stared at him icily and asked where he might put out his cigarette: on one of the paintings, perhaps, or on the floor?

"It's not my problem," replied the lackey. His problem was not to find a solution but to report the facts in the case.

Sergeant Stevens, who had found the exchange amusing, stepped in.

"Let him be, Mark ... Sasta is a very old friend and an expert."

The lackey stared back at Luigi, fixed his loosened tie, and straightened up his shabby suit; but when Luigi stared back at him from the full height of his stocky stature, the lackey left in contempt.

"Do me a favour, Sasta," Sergeant Stevens said. "Butt out your cigarette in here." He handed him a plastic cup, half-filled with cold coffee.

"Why don't you drink an espresso instead of this swill?" Luigi asked him.

"This is standard issue here; maybe you'll offer me an espresso later on ..."

"No, I can't tonight. What was in the wallet?"

"Finish your cigarette, put on your gloves again, and I'll show you the wallet."

Luigi threw his cigarette in the plastic cup, put on his gloves and took the bag with the personal effects. He found a ballpoint pen, a generic American watch from the fifties, a bunch of keys, which Luigi examined, and the wallet. He opened it, noticed the credit cards, an AGO membership card, a library card, a sheet of paper and a folded newspaper article in Italian. Luigi rushed to unfold the article, which was taken from a provincial paper in Lombardy and consisted of an interview with the well-known politician Raul Santamaria, who accused Rome of being a cesspool of vice and corruption.

"I'd like a copy of this article as soon as possible," Luigi asked, even as he was reading it carefully. In the picture Raul Santamaria looked like a lanky, grey-haired and nervous fifty-year-old.

"Do you think it might be a clue?"

"I don't know. "

"What's in the article?"

"It's an interview with Santamaria, a politician who has issues with Rome and talks mostly about technology and jobs ..."

"Can you surmise anything?" asked Sergeant Stevens.

Luigi did not reply but unfolded the brittle, old slip of paper. The ink was almost worn out. Luigi read to himself:

... you are the only person in the world who knows what has always been in my heart, before any other love, and for this I must tell you what is horrible to know: my anguish is borne out of your own, you cannot be replaced, and this is why the life you have given me is condemned to loneliness ...

"What does it say?" Sergeant Stevens asked.

"It could be a poem ..."

"Can it help with the case?"

"Maybe ... I can't tell. If you can get me a copy, I'll have a translation to you by tomorrow. Know anything about the victim's partner?"

"She must already be at the morgue for the identification," Stevens said, handing the poem over to an officer who rushed off and came quickly back with a photocopy.

"What about Carrieri's co-workers, where are they?" Luigi asked, pocketing the photocopy. He folded the slip of paper again and placed it in the wallet, which he dropped into the forensics department's large bag.

"They are all in an office in the gallery but have hardly said a thing. They confirmed that Carrieri had been working, for some time, as a consultant for that institute, that he had no friends, that he was an introvert, albeit a very polite one," said

Sergeant Stevens, relieving Luigi of the forensics bag. "We'll send them home soon."

"Have you seen Tony, my photographer?"

"Yes. Is he ever going to learn English?"

"Never! Tony Camarro speaks the language of the world."

"I see you haven't lost the habit of saying things that mean fuck all." Sergeant Stevens smiled. "I gave him the OK to take some shots in the screening room, but you must promise not to run them ..."

"I am promising nothing," said Luigi, taking his leave of Sergeant Stevens.

He climbed down the stairs and stepped into a room to look at a painting by Dufy, the one Mariuccia had loved so much. He called her Mariuccia but her real name was Mary, Mary Foster. She had been born in Nova Scotia and, like him, loved the sea. The painting was of a yellow piano, and on it, a musical score, whiter than white. His life had been colourless since Mary's death. Too many years had gone by without her, too many since that fateful 1991. He remembered the house he shared with Mariuccia, always filled with flowers, and all the prints of Matisse and Dufy ... He would buy some flowers for Elena.

Chapter 4

"So, how is it?" Elena asked, as she took her place at the table. The room was a little dull, Luigi thought. Light from small but indiscreet halogen lamps fell into the centre of the room, whose walls had been papered over with movie posters. A top-notch professor with two much-discussed books to her credit, and beautiful to boot, which didn't hurt, but above all, his daughter. A small blemish: she lived alone and had no intention of making any changes to her life.

"Delicious!" he replied and, without missing a beat, stuck his fork into another mouthful of stew.

"*Papà*, are you ever going to stop lying?" Elena smiled and topped up his glass with wine.

"Really, Elena; you've outdone yourself ..." Luigi said, setting his fork on the plate.

"Words, words, words ..." Elena hummed to herself, as she got up from the table, basking in the warm glow of two candles. Since her return, Elena had lived in the old house that he had shared with Mariuccia, north of Bloor Street: a small semi on Walmer Road, a crooked riverbed of a street that wended its way to a large clearing, a small piazza resting on a cement foundation covered over with flower beds, with plenty of park benches for the old folks who showed up every morning and evening with their bags of leftover bread to feed the pigeons. To the west, the piazza looked onto a Baptist church that every Sunday overflowed with the music of the black congregation gathered there. To the north, the socialist-realist buildings of the Ukrainian architect Uno Prie exploded into the air from ground level like drunken puffs spewing dirty lumps of coagulated mortar, which had been embellished with syrupy surrealist finishes. The skyscrapers that interrupted the rows of neo-gothic homes covered over by climbing vines seemed like gigantic, arrogant trees growing wild among small quiet vineyards. After Mariuccia had died Luigi had moved back into his parents' house on College Street, just as Elena had done after living for many years in the States. These days she taught at the University of Toronto. All the old furniture was gone; the Scottish sofas, the huge TV and the beds in dark wood had been replaced with pieces from a well-known European furniture chain. Books and posters were everywhere, like in restaurants in the theatre district. Even on the walls of the dining room where Elena had set the table instead of the kitchen. Luigi was at a loss as to what to make of this occasion – was it a formal dinner party for important guests or an intimate supper between father and daughter? Two large blow-ups dominated the room: one was of Jean-Paul Belmondo and Jean Seberg from Godard's film, the other of Chet Baker.

It was nice listening to her talk, hum a famous Italian song from the seventies, but above all it was nice to see her, to share a meal with her. For many years now they had been seeing each other less and less, and always in a hurry.

True, she was busy with her career, but maybe the reason lay elsewhere, which brought on a deep sadness in him, made worse perhaps by the wine, or by the visit with his daughter, the memories, the angina, perhaps by all of these and more.

"What's wrong, *Papà*?" Elena had become concerned with Luigi's silence.

"Your mother used your very same words," Luigi said, his eyes still fixed on the plate.

"Which words?"

"She would always tell me that I lied, but it wasn't true, Elena ..."

"*Papà*, don't start on this again," Elena said, huffing like a teenager.

"And, besides, according to Ibsen the lie is a vital part of life," Luigi continued, but with little confidence.

"That's no reason to lie all the time, like your newspaper ... it's ridiculous ... so out of date," Elena said, leaving the table to tend to the stove.

These words – "that ridiculous newspaper," plus the more humiliating "out of date," – wounded Luigi. He looked over at Elena fumbling with the stove, counted the crumbs on the table, gathered them up carefully with the knife and placed them on the plate, and made as if to get up from the table.

"I must go," he said meekly, moving away from the table.

Elena, holding a cake in her hands, stared at him. "No! You can't leave now, the best is yet to come: the cake I baked, disgusting, I know, but you'll praise it anyway, you'll say it's good, very good indeed," she said, and rudely placed the soufflé on the table.

Luigi stared at the almost shapeless cake, at this soufflé that seemed devoid of any ideals. He sat himself down again with Elena, and together they observed the soufflé as it dramatically exhaled the little air it contained. They looked at each other and burst out in loud laughter.

"Yes! You're so right," he said, approaching her. He embraced her, kissed her hair, and his lips felt the thickness of her blonde curls.

"Even though you were almost bald until you were two years old, you were already very beautiful," he said, breathing in the fragrance of her hair. "I detect a scent of apples and a faint aroma of cigarettes ... maybe not so faint. Have you started smoking again?"

"Stop being a detective, *Papà*." Elena looked at him, misty-eyed. "But you were good, I must say, you were really good, you could have become a famous detective ... but you're right, I started smoking again, two already tonight, and it's your fault because you called me."

"I'm on a new case," he said, returning to his spot.

"I thought that by now," she said, leaning towards him.

"By now?" He glared at her.

"I thought you had no wish to follow any more cases," Elena said sweetly.

"Sergeant Stevens called me. Do you remember him?" Luigi asked her, his eyes now glued on the soufflé.

"Of course I remember him. You were such good friends ... tell me everything," Elena said, settling in her chair.

"Only once I've caught up on your work, on what you do, and if you need anything," Luigi said, looking deeply into her eyes.

"Really? A detective such as yourself who doesn't know what his daughter does?" Elena said, with a dismissive little smile.

"We should never mix work and love, we must always look at things objectively, and as a university professor you should be the first to know that. I could never investigate you ... nor would I ever do it," Luigi said, with a dismissive smile. "Everything is as it should be, *Papà*, don't look at me like that," Elena said.

"What do you mean?"

"That there is no man in my life, that I have no intention of ever getting married and that I have only a casual relationship from time to time."

"I don't want to know anything," Luigi said in a low voice. "It's none of my business."

"OK, let's drop it. Tell me about your investigation."

"Sure ... in any case, I would prefer you did not live alone. It's a very unusual situation, an Italian from Italy, so to speak, and to avoid any ironic twists ..." Luigi felt at ease in this cool house, away from the heat, talking with his daughter about a new murder case, just like they did in the old days.

Mary used to give dinner parties for her friends, who were in love with Luigi and were enraptured with his passionate criticism of Canadian institutions, charmed by his accent. Mary would serve great courses of salmon which they would wash down with white wines from Ontario, but only at the start of the meal; after a couple of glasses Luigi, visibly shaken by abstinence, would run off to his wine cellar for a bottle or two from his private reserve of red wines from Italy. The guests, who had patiently waited for this moment, would finally loosen up into friendly laughter, enjoying the heated debates, not to mention all the compliments in honour of Mary.

"Go on ..."

"Killed with a pointed weapon, possibly a knife with a short, wide blade, a single blow to the nape of the neck while the victim was looking at a screening, a type of movie, at the Art Gallery ..."

"What film?" asked Elena, with mounting interest.

"Three windows of a house in a town in Norway ..."

"Beautiful!" Elena burst out, smiling ironically.

"Joke if you must, but this documentary was part of an exhibition on northern countries. I, too, started looking at it and stood staring at the three windows for a long time ... I feel a little empathy for the victim."

"Watch out, *Papà* ... you don't want to lose your objectivity. What next?"

"Next we found all his papers in his wallet ... a forty-three-year-old man who had anglicized his last name ..."

"I like it already. What else was in the wallet?"

"Credit cards, membership to the AGO, the usual, and a most strange and evocative poem ..."

"What poem?"

"Here is a copy," he said, handing the sheet of paper to

Elena, who stood up, read it carefully and ran off to her room. "And there was something else in the wallet ..."

"What else?" Elena asked in a loud voice, from her bedroom.

"An article cut from a provincial newspaper, an interview with Raul Santamaria."

"Ah, that's a good one! Go on. I'm listening," Elena shouted while she searched her room.

"I think there is some connection with the murder, but I can't really say any more ..."

"I found it!" Elena came back with a book in her hand. "It's a Pasolini poem with the title of '*Supplica a mia madre*,' from the collection *Poesia in forma di rosa*."

Luigi listened as his daughter read.

PRAYER TO MY MOTHER

It is hard to say in a son's words
What I am so little like in my heart.
In the entire world you are the only one who knows
What, before any other love,
My heart always knew.
This is why I must tell you
Something terrible to know:
In your love my anguish was born.
I cannot replace you:
That is why the life you gave me
Is doomed to loneliness.

Luigi and Elena fell silent. She closed the book and sat down.

"Most beautiful," Luigi said, clearing his throat.

"Mafia?" Elena asked, no trace of emotion in her voice.

"I don't think so, does not seem likely, but it's too soon to tell. You're just like Sergeant Stevens ... whenever an Italian is involved the finger gets pointed straight at the Mafia, it's a knee-jerk reaction," Luigi said, unable to mask his irritation.

"Oh *Papà* ... how many Italians with no links to the Mafia have come to a violent death in Toronto?"

"It's just stereotyping!"

"Yeah! Just like it was in 1991, stereotyping!"

"Let's drop it ..."

"Sure, let's drop it, but you did get your chance to clean this city of its stereotypes."

"Easier said than done ..."

"Of course it wasn't easy, but you came very close, you should have brought them to their knees in their underwear, all those sharks, developers, third-rate politicos and priests ..."

"What do priests have to do with it?" Luigi said, going after a slice of soufflé with his fork.

"First of all, they have always been there; secondly, none of them spoke publicly against this scum." Elena got up to go into the kitchen.

"And why should they have?" Luigi asked.

"Because, and you know it very well, the church is really important in the Italian community ... *Radio Redenta* and so on and so on, not to mention the endless number of pages promoting the Vatican in your own paper ..."

"It's not promotion –"

"It is promotion!" Elena cut him off.

"And in any case they would have paid *Signor* Calogero or *Signora* Matilde," Luigi retorted, confirming his long-held suspicion that Elena had inherited Mariuccia's passionate character.

"Who are they?" Elena returned, dangerously wielding a dessert knife.

"They're just names ... your everyday Italians on the street," Luigi replied as he watched his daughter cut up the soufflé and place a slice on his plate.

"Calogero and Matilde ... let's hear it for stereotypes," Elena said.

"In Italy I would have had no scruples, even at the risk of my own life and career – and I beg you to think that I am not lying, but in this country I could not bring myself to use the pages of my newspaper to drag so many honest workers into the mud ... because in the end they would have paid the price," Luigi Sasta retorted, straining to contain his anger.

"Maybe ... but it's also empty rhetoric used to justify all those thieves, all those small-time gangsters financed by governments to pull in votes, all the so-called leaders of the community, all the while chanting the dirge of that poor little saint of an immigrant with his cardboard suitcase."

"It's possible that you see things differently because you're a professor ..."

"Really?"

"You don't have to defend yourself, you don't need to because of your privileged position, but many Italians here have not been fully accepted ...they are still considered ignorant immigrants," Luigi said. "Do you have an ashtray? It's pleasant here, not hot at all ..."

"It's the air conditioning, *Papà* ... These are uncertain times; all of us need to be on guard!"

"Words, words, words," Luigi hummed, getting up to reach the sideboard where Elena kept her port wine.

"At least in this we share the same taste," he said, uncorking the bottle and smelling it.

"Indeed," Elena concurred in a low voice. "What about the murder weapon?"

"There is no weapon, the murderer must have extracted it and discarded it who knows where ... I'll know more tomorrow ... a knife, an awl, in any case an ordinary stabbing tool ..."

"What did this poor devil do? ... In life, I mean."

"He worked in a commercial agency for the Italian

government. Join me?" Luigi asked, pouring some port in his wineglass.

"No, thanks ... OK, just a drop ... what have you written so far?"

"What?" Luigi poured a glass for his daughter.

"What have you written in your paper ... what's it called, again?"

"Come on, don't be coy, you know very well what it's called ..."

"I want to hear you say it!"

"'*Stampa Italica*' ... I have given an exact account of what took place, pointing out that the investigators are groping in the dark; that, while there are many clues, none seem to lead to the Mafia; but I made no reference, perhaps out of respect, to the poem in the wallet ..."

Luigi would have preferred to talk about other things. He had wanted to talk about his angina, about the heart attack that had made him call the ambulance, and about those two weeks of sick leave after so many years of working, without a break or vacation, for a dying newspaper. He had wanted to talk about his personal projects, his wish to start collecting his pension and retire in Italy. What was he doing here in Canada? Why was he not going back to Italy? Mariuccia was dead, and he felt the full weight of her absence in his chest. But Luigi said nothing more; he downed his port in one gulp, kissed his daughter, promising to call on her more often, and left the house for the open air of Walmer Road.

He felt the full violence of the heat, looked back, and saw Elena at the window. He waved goodbye, made a sign that she should go to sleep, loosened his threadbare, pale and lifeless necktie, and walked on. With some relief he noticed the park benches under the lampposts in the small clearing ahead, and tried to reach them. The fear of death had gripped his heart, which was beating violently. He sat down in front of the church, whose austere contours seemed to dissolve and expand like putty being moulded by gigantic hands. He searched frantically for the pills he kept in the inside pocket of his jacket. He opened the pillbox that Mariuccia had given him as a gift in Venice and placed a pill under his tongue. He knew that if one pill didn't work, he would have to take a second one and then a third; and if the three fateful pills would have had no effect, he would have to rush to the nearest emergency room. A couple of minutes went by, and Luigi felt his heart calm down, saw the church regain her solid contours. Only the heat seemed to suffocate him. And it was only at this point that he noticed a man sitting on the next bench scattering breadcrumbs: an old man in a winter suit of blue corduroy, and a felt hat.

"Feeling better?" the old man asked.

"Yes, I think so," Luigi answered, having resisted the urge to light up a cigarette.

"That's the way it is at our age, eh," the old man said, busy crumbling a piece of dried-up bread.

"So it is!"

"Can I do anything for you?"

"No, I'm feeling better ..."

"What is your problem? The heart? The lungs?"

"Angina," Luigi answered.

"Angina," the old man repeated. "The important thing is to want to go on living ..."

"What do you mean?" Luigi asked.

"Look at me ... I am a Polish Jew, born in Poland, landed here a few years after the war, the first one I mean ... so ... can you guess how old I am?"

"You don't look that old," Luigi said, feeling much better now. He gave the old man in front of him a fleeting glance.

"Thanks, but I have been through thick and thin. I finally escaped after I forget how many tries, I have lost track of how much family I have lost, and here I am all by myself ... but everything that's happened to me is locked away here in my heart, who knows all about it and suffers, but not me, I go on."

"It's a beautiful philosophy of life." Luigi smiled.

"You think so? It's not easy, you know ...?"

"And what is your prescription?"

"You make mistakes, and then you fix them."

"Easier said than done."

"Where are you from?"

"Italy."

"I thought so, but come to think of it, who are the real Canadians? I mean, those born here ... how many are they?"

"Not many, and less and less, given that every year there are two hundred and fifty thousand new arrivals, just like us."

"You could speak in Italian if you wish ..."

"Why, do you speak Italian?" Luigi asked, surprised by the old man, who crumbled away at his now very small piece of bread.

"No, but I like listening to it. Italian is the most beautiful language; I am sure it's the language spoken in heaven, and when I die I want to be able to talk with everyone ..."

"Bless you ..."

"You're good people, you've done a great job here, just like the Polish people; we have a lot in common, we are all hard workers and good Catholics ..."

Luigi wondered if the little old man had lost his marbles. In spite of the stifling heat he was dressed in his winter clothes, and only a minute ago he said he was Jewish, now he was saying he was Catholic ...

"But not all of those who came here are like us," he continued. "Take the blacks for example, they don't want to do anything, as soon as they get here they go on welfare ... and what about those stinking Pakistani ..."

Luigi struggled to get up. "Have a good night ..."

"Where are you going?" The old guy went on spreading his crumbs. "The pigeons will come tomorrow," he said.

Luigi had had enough. First an angina attack, then an encounter with a likeable old guy and his eccentric view of life who turned out to be just another diehard racist. What a letdown, in spite of all of his worldly experience! No! Luigi had had it with listening to the same old rants about the same old refugees who had come to Canada to collect welfare cheques and to steal "our" jobs. Just one more proof that we never learn anything, he thought. The poor old guy had escaped from the war, from hunger and probably from the concentration camp, only to wash up thousands of miles away from home making idle conversation on a park bench. He walked to his car, intending to go wandering about on Bloor Street. The night was very young, and he lit up a du Maurier. He saw his own gigantic shadow projected on the wall of the church: he was still alive. No, he thought again, we never really learn anything. The sound of his deep breathing echoed in the street.

Chapter 5
June 6

That morning Luigi was momentarily struck by the odd silence in the newsroom. He was so taken with thinking about the murder at the AGO that he promptly forgot all about this unfamiliar silence and tried to push the door open several times, without success. He tried one more time and it dawned on him that Arazzi, that idiot, was having a little fun pushing back from the other side. Luigi, who was rather heavy, gave the door a strong heave, sending that skinny, balding little satyr flying against a desk. Arazzi regained his composure amidst the laughter of his co-workers, who could barely manage to scream in chorus, *"Surprais!"* Luigi had failed to become accustomed to many things, but he found the North American sensibility that encouraged all staff to see themselves as members of the larger corporate family particularly unnerving. He had never cottoned up to the endless stream of celebrations: birthday parties, welcome parties, goodbye parties, achieved production quota parties, et cetera. Every gesture of affection and gratitude or career advancement was stripped of its private feelings to become a sideshow in a Barnum & Bailey circus of worldliness where all could shed the sweat of their brows in the sacred river of parties.

Arazzi felt right at home in this mindset, which was in keeping with his personal tendency for team-spirited corporate bohemianism. Firm in his belief that he was at the cutting edge of an innovative global journalism, he tried to work his way into the administration as a team leader without arousing feelings of competitiveness. Arazzi kept a running tab on Luigi, noting down all his virtues and blemishes, from his editorial choices to his angina attacks. He sucked in every bit of information for the sole purpose of using it as soon as possible to stab Luigi in the back. Maybe the time had come to pass the mantle to him, Luigi thought, in spite of his natural dislike of the man. And, even though he was convinced that Arazzi was not a good journalist, he knew that he had the necessary dynamism and energy in a country where corporate team spirit reigned supreme.

Signorina Arianna was teary-eyed with emotion, and Luigi pretended to take no notice of her. His wish was confirmed and strengthened by Zavattini's remarks: "Congratulations on a beautiful piece, *Dottore*: you have the right stuff, that's for sure, but don't take it to heart, go easy on it ... easy ... *uonderfùl' articol, uonderfùl'!*"

Luigi was still baffled. It was only when he saw *Signorina* Arianna approach him with a package in her trembling hands while the newsroom team, who in spite of the heat had put on their jackets for the occasion, sang *"eppi bórdai tu iú, eppi bórdai tu iú,"* that he remembered his birthday: sixty-two, to be precise. It was time to retire, as soon as possible. The barista, Giovanni, took the floor.

"Dottore, eppi bórdai! ... Viva l'Italia!"

Amidst the exuberant applause and laughter someone yelled out *"Forza Italia,"* and someone else promptly corrected him with *"Forza Azzurri."*

Luigi was more embarrassed than happy at this uproar in his honour.

"Thank you, Giovanni, *grazie, Signorina* Arianna, thanks everyone," he said. He would have left it at that, but he felt trapped in everyone's gaze; they expected a speech.

Unable to take refuge in his office, Luigi decided to say a few words.

"Thank you for having remembered my birthday, a calendar date that I had completely forgotten." Then again,

Luigi thought, Elena had forgotten too, and he had wanted to tell her that since Mariuccia's death she had never celebrated his birthday, but he would keep it to himself.

"We have been on a long journey together," Luigi started out in his quiet tone, and took a long pause that seemed to hint that a speech about his retirement was coming, on his intention to leave the paper, for health reasons, yes, but above all because, as the director of the paper, he was convinced there was no solid ground to stand on; the hope of a turnaround in the fortunes of *Stampa Italica* was just wishful thinking against the tide of history. As a sixty-two-year-old man with angina, the last thing he wanted was to go against the tide of history. He had done so in his past, but so far back in time that it seemed eons ago, a time when he and Sergeant Stevens were different people. Luigi went on a little longer and was taken aback by his own words.

"But our journey is not over yet. I appeal to your patience, invite you to have faith in your publisher, to believe in *Stampa Italica*, to improve the quality of our reporting, to be present in the community, and to carry on with our pastoral work." (No one laughed, nowadays lapses in the choice of words were easily glossed over, or maybe they just failed to see the irony in his remarks.) "We must reclaim our role as the eyes and ears of the community!" Luigi exclaimed.

"*Amm sorri di mani?*" Tony the photographer said; the staff of *Stampa Italica* looked on in watchful solidarity as he asked for any news about his paycheque.

"Look, guys ... we have two choices ... we stick it out or we go home now!" Luigi replied, happy to have caught the ball in mid-flight, thus deflecting with his ready-made phrase another straight hit by Tony the photographer on the question of unpaid salaries.

Luigi took the gift from the hands of *Signorina* Arianna, who had stood by him, listening rapturously; retired quickly to his office; and collapsed, like a dead weight, on his chair.

He heard the staff chatter on for a while till they broke ranks and returned to their desks. He thought back to last night, when Elena had neglected to wish him a happy birthday. Remembered the last angina attack and the strange meeting with the old Polish Jew ... or Catholic. He talked himself out of lighting a du Maurier; he was in no mood to quit altogether, but he felt he should not overindulge.

He looked at the gift on his desk and noticed a stack of phone messages next to it. They were not piled in chronological order because someone, more than likely *Signorina* Arianna, had placed a message from the Ambassador on top. "Urgent: please call this number ASAP," he read. The President of the Congress of Italian Canadians had also called, and a prominent judge, and a couple of members of Parliament of Italian origin, and, of course, the usual suspects from industry.

Luigi knew too well what they were after, knew their requests by heart: "*Dottore* Sasta, I know you do not need advice from me, but please treat this matter with the utmost discretion, you can imagine how delicate it is, neither of us wishes to turn our community into criminals, so I am asking you to act, as you always have, with extreme tact, and I beg you, if it's at all possible, to keep me in the loop on any developments."

"Don't worry," Luigi would answer. "I will make sure that this information will not be tampered with. Thank you for your phone call, no need to worry, and, yes ... I will keep you in the loop."

He picked up the receiver and asked *Signorina* Arianna to bring him a copy of *Stampa Italica*.

"Today's edition? With your own article, *Dottore*?" asked *Signorina* Arianna.

"Yes, thank you, *Signorina*."

Signorina Arianna came into his office, placed the newspaper on his desk and stood there. He looked up from the front page and was overcome by a feeling of sadness on seeing his deputy editor standing there in her dress of a thousand veils looking like an unemployed fairy.

"Yes? Anything else?"

"Nothing, *Dottore* ... aren't you going to open the gift?"

What gift? Oh, yes, of course ... Luigi unwrapped the package and found a wristwatch, with the title of the newspaper, *Stampa Italica*, engraved on the dial.

"Beautiful!" Luigi said.

"Really?" *Signorina* Arianna asked, with a touch of irony. "I thought you might not like it ... you've written a really beautiful piece ... you know what, *Dottore*, you're wasting your time in this place."

"What do you mean?"

"I meant to say," *Signorina* Arianna backed away towards the door, "that you belong in one of those large Italian dailies ..."

"*Signorina, Stampa Italica* has nothing to envy those dailies, it's just a question of size, but let's drop this ... let's talk about the case. What do you think might have happened at the AGO? I mean who do you think might have killed Michele Carrieri?"

"I have no idea, but it does look like an unusual homicide, with mysterious motives ..."

"Go on." Luigi fixed his intense gaze on *Signorina* Arianna, who, gathering all her strength, added, "Even the murder weapon is unusual, it looks to me like a settling of accounts from the past ... Why had the victim changed his name? This is something we used to do long ago, when Italians were ashamed to have surnames ending in a vowel and had no desire to be singled out."

A silence, like a deep freeze, fell in the room, intimidating *Signorina* Arianna.

"Did I say something out of place?" Signorina Arianna asked fearfully.

"No ... I'm listening, please go on ..."

"An Italian who changes his name has something to hide, something from his past, maybe in Italy, as you yourself hinted at between the lines ..."

"A Mafia killing?"

"I don't think so. Something else, maybe something connected to other motives, ideological maybe ... In Italy all you have to do is cast your fishing line and ..."

Luigi was silent.

"Spying?" *Signorina* asked.

"Maybe ..."

"Politics? Terrorism?"

"Could be, given the age of the victim, or more simply a question of money. Isn't money one of the most common motives?" Luigi asked.

"Of course, you know better than I." *Signorina* Arianna lowered her eyes and backed away from Luigi's desk.

"You know ... but please don't tell anyone ... I found some interesting papers in the victim's wallet ..."

"What did you find?" *Signorina* Arianna approached the desk again.

"A poem and a newspaper article," replied Luigi Sasta. "A poem by Pasolini and an article on Santamaria, the Milanese politician."

"Very strange ..."

"Indeed! In any case, thanks for your thoughts ..."

"No problem, *Dottore*, welcome back!"

"Thank you, *Signorina* Arianna. Talking with you has cleared my mind."

"No problem, *Dottore*," *Signorina* Arianna chirped again as she closed the door and made her way towards the newsroom floating on a cloud, humming.

Sasta took a step or two towards the window, then changed his mind and returned to his desk. He dialed Sergeant Stevens' number but an officer told him he was out of the office. He stood up again, lit a du Maurier and walked back to the window, the same window from which every day he watched the cars lining up at the highway entrance on their way home. Sixty-two years old, forty-four of them at the paper: never a day off, except for illness, as in the past couple of weeks. Should he stay at *Stampa Italica* to the end, endure till the time when the only income would come from the copies sold, till the very last obituary of the very last Italian immigrant?

The publisher came in just then, his face sullen, as usual, with bad news. He had never liked this man of some seventy years, almost completely bald, with thick glasses, prone to profuse sweating (due to his wayward heart) and to an easy optimism that Luigi failed to understand: was it rooted in the self-assurance, in the sense of duty and desperate love of the captain who knows he will never abandon ship, or in the creeping senility of a man who fails to notice that the air conditioning is not working not because it is broken but because he has not paid his bill? In spite of it all, Luigi had stayed put, more out of a sense of duty than of loyalty to the man ... well, maybe both.

"Great piece, Sasta. Well done," the publisher said.

"Thanks," he answered, keeping his eyes glued to the window. When Luigi turned around the two men looked at each other, scrutinizing their aged faces, their gaze dull, without feeling. The heat made them sweat, but the two of them persevered in the trenches. Luigi spoke only to break the silence, not because he had anything to say on the publisher's routine compliment, which was his way of letting Luigi in on his fear that the next article might stray from the placid daily grind.

"No need to worry, I will stick to the specifics of the case, no commentary, but I would like a favour from you ..."

"Sasta, so long as it's not about money, you can ask me for anything," the publisher said, finally cracking a smile.

"No money, just do me the courtesy of calling the Ambassador, I have no desire to speak with him."

"But Sasta, what can I tell him? I am not even following the case."

"But that's why you should call him. You are the right person who can reassure him, calm him down, who can promise to keep him in the loop ..."

"But you'll give me your word that you'll keep me up to date?"

"Yes!"

"I'm in luck, as it turns out! The Ambassador, the Consul and the President of the Congress are all together at the consulate; one phone call will be sufficient ... Sasta, please keep me up to date," the publisher repeated, leaving the office with an optimism that was unusual, to say the least, after these conversations. Luigi hated him, or maybe he didn't.

"Don't worry!" Luigi took his place by the window again.

When the door was finally shut, Luigi Sasta returned to his desk and perused the day's edition of *Stampa Italica*. It was a decent front page: on the left, Mogli's commentary on the upcoming World Cup, on the right, a picture of the Art Gallery with the title, and a re-direct to the full article on page five. That morning at the College Street café, some of the regulars had asked him for his take on the murder at the AGO, but Luigi remained silent, concentrating on the Canadian papers he had been reading. Only one of the dailies reported the homicide on the front page; the rest ran the story on the inside pages, promising to follow it for further developments.

Television newscasts opened with the murder story, giving Luigi a second look at the scene with the crowd loitering about in front of the Gallery. But none of the TV newscasts reported anything of interest.

The phone rang; it was Sergeant Stevens.

"How are you, Sasta?"

"Don't know. Anything new on the murder victim?"

"Squeaky clean criminal record, likely active in student movements of the seventies, at least according to the first reports from your country ..."

"What do you mean by 'active in student movements'?"

"The Italians have sent us some updates on Karrier suggesting that he may have been involved with some terrorist groups ... but they are paranoid ..."

"Left or right?"

Sergeant Stevens's long silence opened a window on that vast desert of ideological categories buffeted by the sudden rise of a desert storm: that old North American fear of communism.

"How should I know? Communist, I'm guessing ... but why would he change his name if his criminal record was clean? ... Unless he was in hiding from someone. The only thing we are sure of is that Karrier had no association with Mafiosi or known criminals ... a total stranger ... unless of course ..."

"Unless?" Luigi barged in on the policeman's musings.

"Unless he led a double life, and if that's the case, it will take a long time to uncover. Any ideas?"

"I'd like to know more about the murder weapon. Have you questioned his live-in companion, what was her name?"

"Valeria Furlon. She dropped in at the morgue last night, identified the body, wept silently; she answered all our questions, saying he had no enemies, here or in Italy ... but she had known him only for the past five years."

"Why had he changed his name? Did she say anything?"

"Only that Karrier wanted to become a full citizen of Canada, that he did not want to be seen as an Italian immigrant, that he wanted to integrate ..."

"A little weak, as explanations go. Have you been to his house?"

"Yes, but we found nothing of interest, just some photos of them together or individual shots. There was one interesting detail. On one of the walls we noticed an impression on the wall, a kind of halo, as if someone had recently removed a framed painting or picture."

"Did you ask her?"

"Yes, apparently it was a print of an abstract painting by an abstract artist."

"I think it was a photograph," puffed Luigi Sasta.

"It's possible. What will you do?"

"What do you mean?"

"What will you write?"

"I have no idea, but for now I would exclude any Mafia killing. Can you fax me a copy of the newspaper cutting that was in Carrieri's wallet?"

"OK."

"Do you think she, this woman, might be involved in the killing?"

"She was at work, lecturing ..."

"And the gallery staff? Anyone with a criminal record?"

"Imagine that ..."

"A crime of passion?"

"There's nothing to go on, and people who knew Michele Carrieri say it's most unlikely."

"I asked my daughter, Elena, to fax you a translation of the poem. Have you received it?"

"Yeah, but I couldn't make heads or tails of it. I don't think it's going to be of any help ..."

"Yeah."

"Keep me in the loop."

Everyone wanted to be kept in the loop. Luigi was confused, grasping at straws. There were no interesting leads up to now. Why had Carrieri changed his name and surname? Who was Michele Carrieri?

Luigi picked up his copy of the newspaper from the desk, lit up a du Maurier and read his messages. They were all still there: the Consul, his Excellency the Ambassador, the Director, the President of the Congress, four or five unfamiliar names – most likely older men who wanted to know who to talk to so they could get their Italian pension – and underneath them all an urgent message from Valeria Furlon asking him to call her. Luigi, startled, dropped his cigarette in the ashtray, placing the newspaper on it. He looked at the phone message and dialed the number. A couple of rings and someone picked up at the other end, without talking. So he started, in Italian: "*Buon giorno*, I am Luigi Sasta, the editor-in-chief of *Stampa Italica*. I am sorry to bother you at such a difficult moment, but I found a message with your name on it ..." His words seemed to fall on deaf ears.

After a long pause a woman's voice answered, "I'd like to meet you, you've written on the murder of Michael and I would like to talk with you without the police being involved."

"Very well, where would you like to meet?"

"Do you know the Beaches area?"

"Yes, I think I know how to get there. "

"Near the end of the neighbourhood, on Queen Street, there is a coffee place, the Golden Gate. You know it?"

"I'll find it."

"How long will it take you to get there?"

"About an hour and a half, we are very far away ..."

"We?"

"I mean the newspaper; our offices are very far away."

"I will only meet with you!"

"Of course! How will I know you?"

"Take a seat at a table and hold the paper wide open. In any case, I know you ..."

"Very well."

"I've seen you many times on television."

Luigi was a little confused as he hung up the receiver. Then he bolted towards the exit; on the desk he had left the unwrapped wristwatch and the newspaper. As he hurried out he heard the fire alarm: the newspaper had caught fire from the cigarette beneath it in the ashtray. Arazzi and Snervato left the building in their usual state of absentmindedness.

"It must have been *Signorina* Arianna. She is boycotting us because we smoke in the newsroom," one of them said. Luigi smiled and quickly left the building, turning around only when he had reached the parking lot. *Stampa Italica* was not going up in flames. That's a shame, he thought, we might have got something from the insurance company. He got into his Subaru, fired up the engine and left the parking lot.

Murder in an exhibition room of the civic museum
ITALIAN MURDERED AT THE ART GALLERY
By Luigi Sasta

The best officers of our police force have been working non-stop since last night in an attempt to solve the mysterious murder of Michael Karrier, a 43-year-old man killed yesterday afternoon at the Art Gallery of Ontario, on Dundas Street. A security guard on his rounds found the body around 2:30 pm. The victim, rigid in the grip of death, was seated on a sofa in a screening room. The first results from the coroner's report on the time and cause of death are of little help to the investigation. Given the setting in of rigor mortis, death was deemed to have occurred a half-hour preceding the discovery of the body, more than likely due to stabbing with a sharp object, a single blow to the nape of the neck with a dagger, or a long knife with a very sharp blade, still to be confirmed by the results of the autopsy. The choice of murder weapon is not the only thing cloaking in mystery the death of Mr. Karrier. Of

Italian origin (born in Milan) but a resident of Toronto for the past fifteen years, Mr. Karrier worked in the offices of an Italian government agency which he left every day at 1 pm for the lunch break, returning at 2:30, then working till 7 pm, when he left to go home.

Before changing his name to Karrier, the victim was known as Michele Carrieri and had been living for many years with a Canadian woman, also of Italian origin. The couple had no children.

The small room in which he was murdered is always kept dark, lit up only by the reflection from the projection screen showing images of a deadly chilling monotony: a fixed focus camera shot of three windows looking out onto the night in a single, interminable sequence. From the loudspeakers, the rhythmic beat of a disco party and the chaotic, shrill cries of seagulls lacerate the small room. The screening room is part of the exhibition Strangers in the Arctic's Ultima Tule, *which is meeting with some success, but given the time of day it was rather empty. The deserted room may explain why the assassin could act with such calm precision.*

The detectives, sticking to their usual discretion, maintain that no hypothesis is to be excluded, not even the likelihood of a Mafia killing. But this theory could be groundless, given that the Mafia's weapons of choice for signature contract killings are of an entirely different category. There are also no grounds to believe that this was a settling of accounts among rival Mafia gangs. As Sergeant Stevens of the homicide squad said to the press: "Karrier could be anything but a Mafia guy."

Who was Michael Karrier? Michele Carrieri could have been a totally different man from the one we know from his daily routine, a man with a double life: the investigators are following this lead.

Chapter 6

Luigi parked on a side street that, under a canopy of wisterias, led all the way to the lake shore. It was a bright, sunny day and the heat was stifling, making it hard for him to breathe. Pale and drawn old men puttered about the front yards that lined the street, pruning and watering their gardens. The bittersweet fragrance of the flowers reminded him of death – and perhaps this was why he had never developed an interest in gardening. For the nth time Luigi tried to understand how a rosebush or flowering plant could be of comfort in old age. In vain.

He reached Queen Street and made for the Golden Gate. A blast of cold air from the AC hit him hard as he made his way inside. It was almost empty save for a stocky, curly-haired guy in a tank top and baseball cap smoking away and drinking his coffee with his gaze firmly focused on the third page of *The Sun*. Luigi walked in, grabbed an ashtray from the pile next to the cash register and sat at one of the tables.

He spread *Stampa Italica* on the table. A waitress approached him to take his order.

"An American coffee," he said distractedly, but really wishing for an espresso.

"Excuse me?" the waitress asked.

"An American coffee!" he repeated.

"Do you mean a Canadian coffee?" she asked.

"Yes, please, a Canadian coffee with cream and sugar."

For health reasons he had cut down on his coffee, but the Canadian/American coffee teased his palate for a cigarette. He shouldn't be smoking, period! But he could not hold a smile back on musing that, in Canada, American coffee was called Canadian, just like in Greece and Turkey, where coffee took on the nationality of the place in which it was ordered.

Who in heaven's name had invented this, whatever it was called, American or Canadian coffee? Who was responsible for this crime? Was it possible that the waitress would not wish to know?

Valeria Furlon put an end to his idle musings. He had no doubt: Valeria Furlon floated down like a queen into suburbia, a luminous, austere apparition in this anonymous dive. Valeria Furlon was dressed in a black linen shift held together by a line of buttons running down from her breasts to halfway down her thighs. Taller than average, about thirty years old, with a lithe body topped by androgynous shoulders on which rested the straps of her dress, short hair framing her face with its large, dark eyes marked by the signs of her recent grief. Pale, fleshy lips and a chiselled chin sculpted by a sure hand, on a long, slender neck embraced by a necklace with a pendant.

"*Signor* Sasta, I am Valeria Furlon."

"*Buon giorno.* Please sit down. Can I offer you something?" Luigi asked.

"Yes, a coffee and one of your cigarettes."

"My pleasure," Luigi said in a bit of a fog, asking the waitress to bring a coffee and mineral water with no ice while offering a du Maurier to Valeria Furlon, who did not wait for him but reached for the matches on the table and lit her cigarette.

"I would have recognized you in any case," Valeria Furlon said in her deep voice, looking at the newspaper spread out in front of them.

"Please excuse me," Luigi said and, in a deeper fog, folded up his paper and put it in his coat pocket.

The waitress walked over with the coffee and mineral water. Luigi and Valeria Furlon remained quiet.

"My condolences, *Signora* Karrier."

Valeria snuffed out her du Maurier in the ashtray and started to talk.

"Please call me Valeria. I called you but I don't even know why I did it. Maybe because you wrote an article asking many questions to which, believe me, not even I have any answers, maybe because you are not a cop, maybe because you can help me because you are Italian and can understand something about Michael that I can't ..."

"Why did Michael change his name?" Luigi asked, clear-headed now.

"Like everyone else you believe that he changed his name out of fear, in order to hide from someone. No, you are wrong, Michael really wanted to become Canadian, he had finally found a home, a homeland ... a woman." She added feebly, "Changing his name meant he could start over from scratch ..."

"Why did he need to start over from scratch?" Luigi asked, his gaze firmly focused on Valeria.

"Because many in Italy are unhappy with the way things are going, and not everyone has been lucky enough to find a new homeland, as Michael did."

"Don't I know it, believe me," Luigi answered, wanting to continue with this line of conversation, but her noble face, unmarked by tears, showed in its paleness the ravages of a sleepless night of intense sorrow that reduced him to silence. Why insist? Valeria knew very well that Michele Carrieri had changed his name for much graver reasons than the weak explanation she had given him, but until the time of his death she had never asked many questions about her partner in life. Time would tell ...

"Do you think that something from Michael's past can shed some light on the reasons for his death?"

"I don't know, but the question posed in your article troubles me as well," Valeria replied.

"You must understand that it's impossible for a man who lived such a normal life to be killed in such a manner." Luigi softened his tone as best he could.

"Michael was a splendid man," she interrupted him, "a man who had suffered a great deal ... I could tell from the look in his eyes, but ... never from his actions. He was the best man for me," Valeria whispered, reaching for the package of du Mauriers, which Luigi handed to her.

"I am not sure, Valeria." Luigi had wanted to add that, from his standpoint, a man who kept a poem in his wallet could hardly be a Mafioso, or even a petty criminal, but this did not mean that he could not have been a man of mystery, tormented by errors from his past. But he did not say anything, perhaps because he no longer thought so or because he thought it was a banal, simplistic explanation. So he lit up a cigarette as well, inhaled a couple of puffs and reflected in silence, noticing a new customer who had looked at them intensely for a moment before sitting down at a nearby table. Luigi's curiosity was piqued and he scrutinized him: he was definitely Latin American, fortyish, dark-skinned, an Asian contour to his penetrating eyes, aquiline nose, thin mouth, short black hair. A brown line suit and matching beige polo shirt hinted at a muscular, lithe, but not too tall, figure. Luigi was at a loss to explain why he feared him.

"Let me help you," Luigi said, turning his gaze to Valeria. "The police have only just started the investigation; many things from Michael's life may be discovered by their research, things you may know nothing about, from his past ... and his present. The most recent present, I mean ..."

"Yes," Valeria said, meekly, "but I want justice! The killer must be punished. Do you understand? Michael was murdered, and justice must be done, the assassin must be punished ... do you understand?"

Valeria's silence prompted Luigi to continue.

"Why had he come to Canada?"

"To start a new life, I've already told you."

"Did Michael ever tell you why he wanted to start over, here in Canada ...? Not many Italians come to Canada these days." Luigi thought back to all the young people who had sought him out, looking for work. "Mass immigration to Canada stopped a long time ago, way before Michael's arrival. Did he have any relatives in Toronto?"

Luigi would have continued, but he was intrigued by the stranger whose gaze was fixed on them till their eyes met, at which point the stranger averted his eyes, and returned to stirring the sugar in his coffee.

"No, no ... Signor Sasta ..."

"Call me Luigi, I beg you ..."

"Michael was the most important man in my life. It's possible that he was just fed up with Italy. He had travelled widely, but he chose Canada because he loved it here, this is where he wanted to set his roots, he wanted to have a child with me ..."

Valeria's voice was broken by the depth of her feelings. Luigi left a ten-dollar bill on the table, gave a last glance towards the Latin American and invited her to go for a walk.

Once out the door Luigi felt the crushing heat press on his chest, taking his breath away, but he withstood the attack. He took off his jacket and wiped his brow with a handkerchief.

Valeria looked at him with some concern, focusing on the sweat cascading from his temples.

"Were you ever a sportsman, *Signor* Sasta? You have the physique of a boxer and also ..."

"The nose ...? No, I've never done much, and I hate boxing ... Valeria, do you think Michael had any enemies here in Canada?"

"No, but I can't exclude it. But certainly not since we started living together. Michael did not see many people."

"Not even a single friend?"

"Not that I know of. He had many acquaintances, but his friends were all abroad, some in Italy, some in Latin America ..."

"Your pendant is Latin American?"

"It's from Peru, it's in turquoise and silver."

"Michael had been to Peru?"

"Yes, and for a long time, but many years ago."

Work in progress along the sidewalk forced them to cross the street, and they walked along the lakeshore, on Queen Street, in the direction of Scarborough. The noise of a nearby jackhammer tormented Luigi Sasta's temples as he stopped to look behind him, to check if the stranger from the Golden Gate was following them. Was it possible that Valeria had not noticed him? At this hour on Queen Street you could only come across a few retired people and women pushing baby carriages.

"Valeria, did you come by yourself? Did you bring a friend?"

Valeria Furlon gave him a questioning look. "No, why would I do that?"

Luigi checked again and continued.

"And in Italy? Who were his friends in Italy?" he asked, walking again beside her.

"I've already told you that I don't know."

"Have you been to Italy with Michael?"

"No!"

"Valeria, were you aware that in Michael's wallet ..." Perhaps out of respect for Valeria, Luigi could not bring himself to refer to the victim by his real, Italian name. "The detectives found an article from an Italian provincial newspaper ... an interview with a politician, a certain Raul Santamaria. Any idea who he might be?"

"No, it doesn't ring a bell."

"Do you know if Michael belonged to Santamaria's political party?"

"I don't think so, really; Michael had shut the door on Italy." Valeria added, noticing Luigi's scepticism, "He never stopped talking about that."

"Then why, from your point of view, do you think an Italian who lives in Canada would carry such an article in his wallet?"

"Maybe because he was as interested in the politics of his home country as he was in Canadian politics ..."

"But I thought he had shut the door on Italy ...?"

"He had no desire to live there, but Michael was interested in everything."

"The article is from a year and a half ago. Other than his office work, what did Michael do with his life? Any hobbies, interests?"

"Yes, he read travel books and poetry."

"Did he keep a journal?" Luigi asked.

"No, look, *Signor* Sasta, you're really on the wrong track ..."

"Then please help me get back onto the right track. One of the detectives told me that a painting or photograph is missing from your house. The shadow left by the frame is still on the wall."

"I told the police that it was a painting."

"Of what?"

"A Rothko print."

"Who?"

"Rothko, an American painter; neo-expressionist, abstract."

"What was in the painting?"

"Three coloured rectangles on a black background."

"That's it?"

"Yes, you can see it if you want at ..."

"The Art Gallery!"

"Yes," Valeria answered, and became suddenly silent as

they reached the lake at the foot of the hill of the R.C. Harris Water Filtration Plant.

Luigi felt tired. "Can we stop for a while?" he asked.

"You don't feel well?"

"Nothing to worry about, just old age ..."

Valeria sat quietly down on the grass. Luigi looked up at the sun, breathing in the fresh breeze that rose up from the lake. The stark filtration plant, austere as an abbey, dominated the hillside meadows on which it stood. Valeria and Luigi were the only living beings. The huge windows of the building, the colour of the water, gave Luigi the impression that they had landed at an ancient temple bordering on the Mediterranean.

Valeria started again: "We came here frequently. This was Michael's favourite place. He would often say that the lake was as large as Lake Titicaca, looking out to the horizon, dreaming of one day going to live together in the real Canada."

"Why the real Canada?"

"Because for him Toronto was not Canada, the land of deep silence, of our primal past. Toronto was a city of the future, a city of all races and cultures, like Milan, his own city, where you breathe in tension and violence with your first breath ..."

Luigi opted for silence.

"For Michael," Valeria added, "Toronto did not represent Canada, and he wanted to go into the most faraway Canada. Did you know that only a year or two ago Aldo Rossi had planned to build a theatre here? For me this is one of the strangest places, so different, the architecture, nature ... When Michael's body is returned to me I'll have it cremated, that's what he wanted ... and will spread the ashes here."

Luigi could not muster up the courage to ask who Aldo Rossi might be, and his mind wandered to Mariuccia; he wanted to be buried next to her, in the cemetery on St. Clair Avenue; to think that he often told her he did not want to die in Canada, that he wanted to be buried on a hilltop in the

Marches region. Who would show up at his funeral? Elena, maybe, and *Signorina* Arianna for sure, Sergeant Stevens, and one or two staffers from *Stampa Italica*, the Ambassador, maybe, but more likely the consul general. He wished that the publisher would not be present, and that Arazzi would not be entrusted with doing the eulogy.

He decided to take a nitroglycerin and placed a pill underneath his tongue, making sure not to be noticed by Valeria.

"Michael would often say that you were the only journalist who wrote the truth about things, that you were fearless in your approach ..."

Luigi remained quiet.

"He had wanted to meet you ..."

"And why would he want to meet me?"

Luigi's question went unanswered. They were distracted by the noise coming from a car angrily roaring into the space at the bottom of the hill. Valeria grabbed his arm, but her grip caused him pain, as this was the arm that registered pain during an angina attack. In the driver's seat he noticed the strange customer who had scrutinized them at the Golden Gate.

Luigi and Valeria felt no need to talk. They started on their climb back up to the filtration plant but had to take the hill, as the road was blocked by the car of the Latin American. While helping Valeria, Luigi turned around and saw the angry face of the stranger, who was now climbing towards them at a quick pace. There was no way Luigi could outrun him; his pace had slowed down and he moved slowly, hoping that the nitroglycerin would kick in.

"We have to hurry!" Valeria cried out.

"Go on, run, go without me, don't worry, go," Luigi said feebly as he let himself down on the grass, where he sat looking on, almost without any feeling, as the Latin American climbed effortlessly up the hill, one hand in his pocket.

"Take the phone from my jacket and call 911," Luigi said.

Feverishly, Valeria fumbled in the jacket for the cellphone, grabbed it and dialed the number. The Latin American stopped halfway up the edge. He had a fierce look in his eyes.

"Please get up, *Signor* Sasta!"

"I can't."

Valeria took his arm and helped him up. Luigi put his arm around her neck, and together they reached the entrance of the R.C. Harris Water Filtration plant.

Valeria pushed the door open and helped Luigi inside the building. He thought he had ended up inside the pump room of the *Nautilus*; the water filtration machinery looked like compressors in a submarine, and he half-expected to see giant octopuses and marine monsters in the huge windows. A man in a white lab coat approached them. Valeria shouted at him, asking for help.

"We are waiting for the police. Please help me. This man is ill!" She turned to look at Luigi and spoke to him sweetly. The nitroglycerin pill was kicking in. Luigi pulled away from Valeria's arm; his energy was slowly returning and, despite an extreme tiredness and the pain in his chest, his arm and his back, he managed to step outside. The sun was still beating down. The Latin American had vanished, but a police squad was approaching. He made his way back inside.

"The police are here but the stranger is gone," he said. Valeria looked at him with terror-stricken eyes. "Now you will tell me the truth!"

Chapter 7

That afternoon, in the police car, Luigi went home with Valeria to her house in the Beaches area. He called Sergeant Stevens, and they decided to meet later in the evening in front of the monument to Simón Bolívar in a park in the Portuguese neighbourhood.

Once the police had left them at Valeria's front door, she invited him inside; Luigi wavered before walking into the home of a murder victim. Valeria, worried about his state of health, insisted that he come in for a strong drink. Luigi, won over, walked into the house but could hardly contain his curiosity until he was left alone in the room so he could make his phone call to Sergeant Stevens in private.

Shelves, overflowing with books, lined up the walls. Below the windowsill the sofa was buried in piles of photographs, magazines and records. Valeria had informed him that the police had turned the place inside out looking for God knows what, finally walking away with several of her books and some of .Michael's. At worst, this gave the police the opportunity to read something intelligent, Valeria had said, moving into the kitchen. Luigi smiled, put his cellphone away and, taking his time, stepped over to the sofa and glanced at several photographs. He was struck by the fact that they were all of the same subject: Valeria, all smiles, and in every pose imaginable; on stage behind the scenes, in a billiard parlour (New York, maybe?), in silhouette against a lake (Harris Filtration Plant, maybe?).

In some photos she was seen embracing Michael Karrier on that same sofa, a cigarette hanging from his lips, in his pyjamas, his hair all messed up. He saw many others showing the two of them in their travels: Michael in a canoe on a river, Michael talking with a traffic officer in a city that reminded him of Milan. Luigi moved closer to the shelves, checking the titles, many of which were in Italian. He was not yet clear on what he was looking for and felt a sense of guilt, as though he was betraying Valeria's trust by rummaging through that vast collection of titles that seemed to contain all of the comings and goings of Michael Karrier's daily life. His curiosity was piqued by a single title, *An Atlas of Fantasy*; on the fly-leaf of the back cover, he read Valeria's dedication of the book to Michael Karrier:

May 6
New places to see together.
Love,
Valeria

Leafing through the book, Luigi noticed many maps of imaginary and mysterious places, with names to match: *Schlaraffeland, The Land of Mice, Oz, Quivira, Baesoom Simrana* ...Valeria came into the room. Luigi placed the book back on the shelf and followed her into the kitchen, sat down at the table and looked out the window facing her backyard. Having completely covered the surrounding walls, the climbing plants held the house in a cool, green embrace.

Valeria and Michael Karrier had nested here in this mysterious cocoon, living so near and yet so far from the world.

Luigi offered her a cigarette, which she accepted, and Valeria poured him a whisky.

"Whose book is that?" Luigi broke the silence.

"Which one?"

"The *Atlas of Fantasy*."

"I told you, Michael loved travel books ..."

"But these are non-existent destinations."

Valeria was quiet for a while, before returning to their conversation.

"I'll tell you everything I know, which is not much, but you must help me to get justice done."

Luigi was quiet, his gaze fixed on Valeria. She talked for the longest time, while they smoked the whole pack of du Mauriers. Finally, overcome with exhaustion, Luigi pleaded with Valeria to be very, very careful. On his way out she took his hand in hers and held it for a long time in silence. He pulled away, confused, and urged her to get some sleep. Wearily he walked over to his car, sat behind the wheel of his old Subaru, and was greeted by a blast of extremely hot air. He gripped the blistering steering wheel, turned the key, fired up the engine and drove himself home. On the way he dialed the number of *Stampa Italica* and spoke with *Signorina* Arianna, giving her a heads-up that by day's end he would be faxing a couple of pieces. *Signorina* Arianna promised to run them on the front page. Luigi asked if there was anything new, and *Signorina* Arianna reassured him that nothing new had taken place, save for the ongoing litigation with the landlord of the *Stampa Italica* building, and consequently there was still no air conditioning.

Luigi took his leave quickly, closed his cellphone, relaxed his body against the backrest of the car seat, drove along Queen Street and turned in to the racetrack. The empty rows of seats in the blinding sunlight, the vacant parking lot, and that singular desolation of deserted entertainment venues reminded him of evenings when he and Mariuccia squandered their few dollars betting on favourite horses; hot tips given to Luigi by Valenti, an Italian jockey who had found success in Toronto. Who cared if Blue Sky or High Fever turned out to be losers, as Valenti's tips were always wrong. Luigi recalled those hazy, hot nights from long ago, nights before his angina (that cursed angina!), when the heat did not bother him. And now, here he was at the end of a long road, unmarked by his passage, no trace of his having stood out in any way, no flashes of genius, no sudden breaks from the pack. True, he had broken into gallop on occasion ... but that was before '91. What had happened in '91?

When he tried to summon up the memory of that time, the days rose up in an endless parade without history or incident, unchanging, year after year, till he became numb to it all: especially to his painful realization that his daughter may have personally thought him a loser, a coward; to his work in a newspaper whose days were numbered; to his life in a community in which he felt more estranged every day; to a city he longer considered his own. Had it ever been his city? He recalled a feeling of citizenship, of belonging to this city when he thought back to Mariuccia spurring Valenti, whooshing past, airborne on his saddle, on to victory, with Elena blessedly asleep, smiling in her arms.

When Sergeant Stevens exposed the exorbitant spending sprees of a few councilmen subsidized by some "Lords of Cement" and Luigi hurried to *Stampa Italia* eager to write his piece about it, he felt like he was cleaning up his community of its ills. This is the real community I belong to, Luigi thought: no one in particular, no leader, no judge, no member of Parliament, no benefactor, no publisher; many nameless but not faceless people that you could meet working as caretakers in the schools, paving the city streets, on construction sites, resting on benches along College Street, going to church at dawn. A passionate community of outsiders, of hard-working people, honest to a fault, washing away its scars and diseases in the waters of the great Ganges of this new world.

Michael had been a regular reader of his articles, which he loved, Valeria had told him. Luigi recalled the photographs of Valeria embracing Michael, a dreamer who thought he could change his life by merely changing his name: there was no hiding from the past, no safety in running away from it, it always pulled you back. Maybe that was the reason he felt some sympathy for the delusional Michael Karrier, who carried a Pasolini poem in his pocket on his walks to the Art

Gallery. Michael might have been killed because he wanted to wipe the slate clean on his past. The more Luigi reflected on this the more certain he became; he was sure of it, in spite of the lack of a motive.

Luigi arrived home, parked his car in the garage and entered into the house; thankfully, the air conditioning was working. He removed his jacket and tie and put on a t-shirt, stepped into the kitchen, opened up a can of juice and walked into the living room. He would have preferred a beer. The house was dark; he stretched out on the sofa and closed his eyes. He recalled the Latin American approaching him menacingly with the confidence of an agile and determined predator. This made him even more tired. He had not been afraid for himself; rather, he was worried about Valeria. From the start he had liked this girl so determined on defending her partner. She reminded him of Elena's fearlessness. He got up, climbed the stairs to his bedroom, undressed meticulously, chose a pyjama set from his chest of drawers, put it on and lay down on the bed.

Sergeant Stevens had warned him to be careful, but of what? He was pleased that his old friend was concerned enough to warn him, in spite of a broken friendship for which they shared the blame, their lack of drive. We are always running about, but how often can we win? Luigi asked himself, and once again he saw Mariuccia running happily to the wicket to collect her winnings, Elena still asleep in her arms. He closed his eyes.

Chapter 8

On the verandas of houses lining up Grace Street, old men in unbuttoned shirts, which they wore over immaculate undershirts, slouched on old chairs or sat on the front steps gazing into the void, taking in the invasive Latin beat coming from a car parked in front of the elementary school. Leaning against the car door were two youths in tank tops, quietly idling away their time. Luigi made his way along the street. It was about eight-thirty in the evening and even though there was no sign of the heat cooling down, he felt much better and his swift pace caused him no shortness of breath. He had slept for five hours, and woken up in a good mood, and even in good health. In the schoolyard a few Chinese teenagers sat on the grass playing cards while nearby a couple of infants, helped by their parents, were taking their first steps and emitted little cries of wonder at the flight of seagulls overhead. Luigi put aside any thoughts of what had happened that morning, basked in quiet solitude before the summer night set in, and got ready, with enthusiasm, for his meeting with Sergeant Stevens. He longed for a du Maurier, but remembered his doctor's warnings and took in a deep breath that filled his lungs with a stinking whiff of grilled fish that almost choked him. This came from the backyard of one of the houses on the street, where families cooked their summer fare with garlic cloves the size of oranges, and washed it down with bottles of homemade wine. A young family – father, mother and two children – were leaving the Portuguese church and stopped on the corner to buy ice cream from the ice cream truck. Luigi watched the father, brooding and thoughtful, count the bills. The summer brought work to many in this neighbourhood; well-paid work in construction, where shifts started at six in the morning and went on till nightfall. He turned around, like someone who senses he is being followed, and noticed College Street crowding with long lines of people exiting from restaurants and cafés, mingling together before going in opposite directions.

Luigi went in the other direction, towards the park. Encouraged by the peace and quiet of the summer evening, he attempted to reconstruct the events of that afternoon. Now he grasped the full extent of the risk he had faced and became concerned above all for Valeria's safety. Michael Karrier had changed his name to go into hiding, and it was clear that his enemy or enemies were on the lookout for him. Now that he was out of the way they would also kill Valeria, who may not have known anything, but neither Luigi nor the assassin could be sure of it.

While it was possible that the Latin American could have been the killer, Luigi put this idea on the back burner in favour of a friend or enemy that Michael Karrier had met on his trips to South America.

Stevens, seated on a bench right in front of the statue of Simón Bolívar, was waiting for him. Luigi crossed the street, cutting in front of a van carrying a group of Indians who had finished their rounds of distributing advertising materials in the neighbourhood. Advertising agencies hired them early in the morning and dispatched them in little-known areas of the city where they stuffed mailboxes full of flyers offering fabulous discounts on legs of lamb, computers and detergents. Luigi sat down on the bench and let out a loud sigh.

"It's hot," Stevens observed as he watched a crowd of young people weave in and out of the traffic looking for restaurants on College Street.

"It's deadly," said Luigi, without a hint of irony.

"It's been years since we have had this weather. When I was a kid in Toronto summers weren't so hot, and in winter there was much more snow and it was colder ... I guess this is the effect of global warming ..."

"Could be," Luigi agreed. "What's new?" he asked, if only to put an end to the idle talk of two old geezers sitting on a park bench looking on a world going by, absolutely indifferent to their growing older.

"Nothing. We haven't been able to find anything on the Latin American, other than the fact that his profile matches about a thousand other Latin Americans."

"I'm sorry I did not get his name," Luigi said. He could not hold back anymore and lit up a du Maurier.

Sergeant Stevens looked at him quizzically. "You've always been like this ... such a strange sense of humour ..."

"You should talk. Every joke you crack smacks of criminal intent – racism, to be clear," Luigi remarked, even though he knew he was wasting his time.

"Don't tell me you've become a radical? You've always been at it; don't you ever get tired of saving the world?" Sergeant Stevens scolded him. "In any case, we haven't been able to find any clues. You mentioned on the phone that you've found the murder weapon?" asked Sergeant Stevens, coughing violently.

"Great cough for a guy in retirement," Luigi remarked.

"Look who's talking. Would you mind moving your cigarette away? You're polluting me," the Sergeant retorted.

"To tell the truth, I think I have discovered many things today. Valeria was terrified after today's event, and I have no doubts that she did not know everything concerning Michael Karrier ..."

"Michele Carrieri, you mean." Sergeant Stevens looked at him, his curiosity piqued. "Go on ..."

"Yes, I don't think she knows much about Michele Carrieri, or, more precisely, about her partner's past life in Peru, for example, where he lived for a long time with friends who loved bullfighting –"

"Which friends?" asked Sergeant Stevens.

"Hang in there ... listen ... the murder weapon could be a *puntilla* or *puntillo*, a type of dagger used to finish off the bull when he is almost dead. The Latin American, the Peruvian, is a friend of his ..."

"How do you know this?" Sergeant Stevens jumped to his feet.

"After today's events, I put some pressure on Valeria, but I must also tell you that in the past I was a fan of bullfighting. Have you ever seen one? More often than not, it's not the matador's sword that kills the bull that's been bleeding for the longest time but a thrust of the *puntillo*; a clean stab to the base of the skull and the bull is struck dead. Generally it is a butcher ... I am convinced that Karrier was killed by a professional, not necessarily a hired killer, but someone who knew what he was doing in terms of timing and method." Luigi threw his cigarette butt on the ground and it landed next to Stevens, who snuffed it out with his foot.

"Will she work with us?" Sergeant Stevens turned to face him.

"I'm not sure to what extent. She loved him," Luigi said.

"Valeria is our only source of information. Karrier was killed in the Art Gallery, and today the murderer, who must be the same person, attempts to kill her, and you as well ... and we are left in the dark. The only clue we have is that the murder weapon could have been a type of dagger used in bullfighting. It's not much ... and to top it all off, we must be gentle with the victim's partner ..."

"There is another possibility." Luigi followed the thread of his own thoughts and paid little attention to Stevens's complaints, who turned to face him, deeply concerned. Luigi noticed he was getting fat: so much time had gone by, and they had reached pensionable age; better to take retirement than to chase after killers.

"What will you do when you retire?" Luigi asked out of the blue. Stevens swore at him, signalling that he get off his idiotic train of thought and back on track.

"The possibility," Luigi started again, "is that the murder weapon has a symbolic meaning: Karrier was punished for betraying someone." He fumbled in his pocket for the package of du Mauriers. "Let's say, for example, that Karrier goes to Peru, and together with his friends, takes an oath to never disclose a shared secret, on pain of death, and should he fail to keep it, he will be killed in a style showing his infamy. Since they are all fans of bullfighting, they adopt the *puntillo* as the weapon of choice for the final punishment ... a type of death and murder using a weapon with special meaning for them ..."

"It smells too much of Sherlock Holmes ... but why did they kill him?" Sergeant Stevens grimaced in puzzlement. "Must we check out every Peruvian in Toronto?"

"There can't be that many. He may have come from out of the country. I would check out the border crossings, flights, train and ship arrivals, bicycles ... all! Let's go ... come on, let's take a walk in the park." Luigi inhaled deeply on his du Maurier and stood up from the bench.

Sergeant Stevens and Luigi crossed over to the park, where some dogs were barking, happily chasing each other under the watchful eyes of their owners.

"Did you know that a river flowed underneath here?" Luigi asked Sergeant Stevens, who seemed to be daydreaming.

"Yes. I heard about that and have some vague memory of it ..."

"Really! I doubt it! The river was covered up at the end of the last century, so unless you are over a hundred years old ... but maybe you are telling the truth about your memory of it ..."

"What do you mean?" Sergeant Stevens stopped walking along the path and fixed Luigi in his gaze.

Luigi flashed him a cryptic smile. "Nothing important ... our only investigative lead points firmly at the Latin American. It's the only clue we've got. If he had not attempted to kill us today or threaten us, we would have little if anything to go on, and the case would be shelved ... but the Peruvian has a name –"

"Really?" Sergeant Stevens jumped in.

"Yes, he is known as Lucio Marros," Luigi Sasta volunteered, icily.

"Why didn't you tell me from the start?"

"Let's stay on track here ..."

"How did you find it?"

"From Valeria Furlon, obviously ..."

"Well, in that case I'll have her summoned to my office so she can explain everything, starting with the miraculous recovery of her memory!"

"Don't do it, Stevens!" Luigi stopped and, looking at Sergeant Stevens, added, "Don't waste your time, she's got nothing more on this."

"All right!" Sergeant Stevens grumbled, not fully buying it. "Go on ..."

Luigi regained his breath. "Lucio Marros, whatever his name, appears in the picture ... he's a Peruvian bullfighter."

"What does Valeria Furlon know? What does Karrier's murderer believe Valeria knows?"

"Let's take that picture," Luigi said in a flat monotone.

"You keep harping on some picture. What picture?"

"Remember what you told me after you searched Valeria Furlon's house, about the outline of a missing frame from a wall? There had been a picture on that wall, a photograph of Michael and some friends from Milan: Raul, Tino and Beppe ... and guess where they are in that picture?"

"In Peru!"

"They're in Lima, and Marros is in the picture with them."

"Did she tell you all this?" Sergeant Stevens asked as he kicked a soccer ball back to some kids.

"Yes!"

"So where is the picture?" Sergeant Stevens asked, wiping his shoe with one of his hands.

"Valeria Furlon believes Karrier threw it out."

"So you think we should leave Valeria Furlon out of this in the hope that Lucio will turn up looking for the picture ..."

"More or less. Do you know who one of the friends in the picture was?"

"Tell me!" Sergeant Stevens stopped once again in the middle of their path, looking at Luigi.

"Raul Santamaria, leader of a political party in northern Italy who – but I see you've already figured it out ..."

"He's the man pictured in the article we found in Karrier's wallet!"

"Exactly! When I showed her the article found in his wallet, she recognized him."

"Valeria Furlon knows a great deal more than she admits ..."

"Not to worry." Luigi took Sergeant Stevens by his arm, pushing him towards some trees, where they rested in their shade.

"But how can we prove that there is some connection between the victim and this guy?" Stevens asked.

"We can't prove it," Luigi said, looking at the tennis courts in the distance where some teenagers were playing, "unless we get our hands on the picture ..."

"Why did the Latino try to kill Valeria Furlon? And how did he know about the picture?"

"Well, why don't we begin by checking if Santamaria ever came to Canada to visit with Karrier, or if either of the two friends, Tino or Beppe, ever came to Toronto, or if they came all together ... because if Santamaria or his friends knew of the picture, they will try to wipe out any evidence that will lead to them."

"Have you asked Valeria Furlon?" Sergeant Stevens tore off a large leaf from the oak tree and brought it to his mouth, sucking on the stem.

"She claims she's never met any of them, and I believe her ..."

"Why?"

"Because she is truly in love with Karrier, and for this reason alone I believe she has no desire to defend the assassins ... she just wants to defend Michael ..."

"You like this girl, don't you?"

"Yes ... and you?"

"She's just a snob, another radicalized professor ..."

Luigi held back a sneer. "It's possible that the Latino had planned to kill only Michael, then things got complicated with Valeria Furlon, and that picture ... let's assume that someone must have seen that picture, say Santamaria on a trip from Milan to Toronto. Can you check that out?"

"Seems far-fetched to me," grumbled Sergeant Stevens.

"You're right, it is far-fetched, but we have no other clues. What say you we go for a drink?"

"OK, but where is the picture?"

"I've already told you: as far as Valeria Furlon knows, Karrier threw it away."

"I think she has it."

"And where would she keep it?"

"I haven't got a clue. Maybe she gave it to a friend or maybe Karrier has hidden it ... don't know where ..."

"If that picture is still around we must find it, for Furlon's safety. In the meantime you could check up on Santamaria ... and on Lucio."

They walked through the Queen Street gates, leaving the park behind them, and hailed a taxi. Evening was falling, and with it came the promise of cooler air, though neither of them believed it. They took their seats in the taxi, driven by a Somali with zero knowledge of city streets, and rolled down the windows. Sergeant Stevens patiently called out the directions to the driver.

"Nowadays anyone can get a taxi licence," he said, turning his sullen gaze beyond the window. On the way, they talked about their retirement and travel plans. Sergeant Stevens hoped to go to Florida, Luigi to Italy.

Turning to Sergeant Stevens, Luigi became sentimental. "Isn't Toronto just marvellous? Where else would you find a Somali who speaks Italian better than an Italian?"

"Only thing I know is that he has no idea how to get there and it will cost us double," Sergeant Stevens said sourly in response, which made Luigi smile. He asked the driver if he could smoke.

"You never refuse anything to an Italian, Italian Mafia," the driver said with a broad smile.

"I'm starting to like this guy," Sergeant Stevens said.

Luigi lit up a du Maurier.

Chapter 9

Luigi left the bar, picked up his cellphone and called *Stampa Italica*. Arazzi picked up.

"How are you, boss?"

"When are you going to stop calling me 'boss'?" Luigi said. "Any news?"

"Yes, Italy will win the World Cup, but that's old news ..."

"Other news?" Luigi Sasta asked.

"Not that I am aware of. Would you like to talk with *Signorina* Arianna?"

"Yes, thank you."

Looking back into the bar, Luigi saw Sergeant Stevens eating his stewed fruit. Then he heard *Signorina* Arianna's voice.

"Yes?"

"*Signorina*, it's Luigi ..."

"How are you, *Dottore*?"

"I'm well, thank you. Any news? Have you received my pieces?"

"Yes, well done *Dottore*, the puzzle is coming together ..."

"Looks like it is ... but we still have a long way to go. We have to find a reason ... we don't have a motive."

"True. No one called for you, except one or two of the Canadian dailies asking for a comment from you on this story."

"Please tell them I have no intention of making any comments," he answered tersely. Valeria's tired and pained face flashed before him. "Anything else?"

"Nothing, save for the paycheques ..."

"Don't you jump on this tired old bandwagon. We have to hold on tight ..."

"You're right, *Dottore* ... you know my loyalty ..." *Signorina* Arianna fell silent for the longest time, which Luigi found unbearable. "But the others, our colleagues, are complaining. They are fond of you and don't want to say anything directly, but they can't take it anymore, and some want to take the matter up with the unions ..."

"I know. How are we laying out the front page?"

"With the national soccer team and with your piece, 'New Leads', et cetera ..."

"Very well ... I'll see you tomorrow, *Signorina*."

"For sure, good night, *Dottore,* and take care."

"Thank you."

Luigi closed his cellphone and returned to sit with Sergeant Stevens, who was busy ladling up the remaining pieces of stewed fruit.

Do you remember the last time we came here? They both wanted to ask this of each other. But neither spoke.

After so many years fate had brought them together again (Luigi was very grateful that Sergeant Stevens had called him after such a long silence), offering them the opportunity to work together on a case. This time there was no room for cold feet or intimidation. The truth must be unveiled, if only to close shop with a modicum of decency. They both knew it.

"Some dailies called my news desk asking for developments. They wanted to speak to me." Luigi lit up another du Maurier.

"You declined?"

"Of course I did," Luigi said. He was about to add that he did not wish to give out any information until he had a chance to go over some details with Valeria, but he was interrupted by the waitress.

"I'm sorry, sir, but this is a non-smoking zone," she said politely.

"But there is no one here at this time to be offended by my smoking."

"This is the law, sir. I assure you I didn't make it."

Luigi turned his pleading eyes to Sergeant Stevens.

"Luigi, it's the law!" he said, laughing.

Luigi looked sadly at his cigarette and asked for an ashtray. The waitress promptly supplied one. Luigi took one last puff of bluish smoke before angrily snuffing out his cigarette.

"Stevens, this time I will get to the bottom of this, and there is no one to stop me," Luigi blurted out point-blank before calling out loud, "The cheque, please!"

They stood up, left the place, shook hands and went their separate ways.

"Be careful!" Sergeant Stevens offered.

"Someone else better be careful!" he answered. Luigi turned away from the Sergeant and set out on the sidewalk flanked by cars waiting for the red light to change on their way to Little Italy.

Chapter 10

Luigi walked by the crowded cafés before stopping at the entrance to Bar Italia, a temple devoted to the ethno-jazz lifestyle of College Street. A couple of speakers on the patio blared their music to the sidewalk. Weary, bored faces of young people looking out from the window were reflected in Luigi's tired gaze. Luigi caught his own reflection in the window, his curiosity piqued by a sudden glimmer in his hair that made him look younger. For the first time after so many years Luigi scrutinized his image with icy precision, with the analytical detachment of the reporter-detective or detective-reporter that had been his trademark. Miraculously all his hair was still in place, and even more miraculously there were signs of greyness only around his temples. He was stocky, though he was taller than average, but had never been a boxer as everyone assumed due to his misshapen nose. Naturally, he was not lacking a pot-belly, but this was due to his age, not to a runaway passion for food. Luigi continued his dissection: large bags rested placidly in wide circles under his eyes, his nose had certainly grown larger and his lower lip had relaxed into a mandibular protrusion, giving him the look of a very sad mastiff. All was as it should be: Luigi Sasta was a sad man, and now he felt the full weight of it. On this busy street where taxis and cars unloaded youthful couples and aging, pensive intellectuals in the company of silent and ethereal muses, Luigi, grey and rundown, walked all alone, grappling with nostalgia.

Following the rhythm of scheduled shift work, older Italians and Portuguese residents retired to their living rooms to watch television or play cards in their backyards, while a newer fauna took over College Street. Strong, greasy gusts of grilled meat and pizza blew over from the bar and grill on the corner to the tune of a different type of music, while throngs of customers took their turns at the tables for a beer, a *granita* or a gelato. All around him the night was bursting with intense bright joy, but Luigi's mind was clouded by thoughts of Valeria alone in the house where she had lived happily in ignorant bliss with Michael Karrier. He thought, or imagined, that all the suffering that Michael endured from his life's wounds, including his own remorse, had not been enough: in the end he was slaughtered by the hand of the Peruvian. Luigi had no doubts about this. In spite of the few clues, he was certain that Michael Karrier had been killed for wrongs he had committed in Latin America or in Italy, places of history and blood, which amount to the same thing. He thought of Orson Welles's reply to Joseph Cotten's question on why there is so much blood and murder. With pointed irony, Welles reminded him that during the Renaissance men murdered and poisoned each other, and asked him to think on the outcome of all the spilled blood, the murderous plots: great works of art and culture, while Switzerland, with all its peace and quiet, its lily-white purity, had only given us the cuckoo clock.

Poor Michele Carrieri! He had come to Canada to start a new life, even though he must have known that you can never run away from the past; you can turn over a new leaf, you can modify it, but the past will hunt you down mercilessly. Poor Michael, who kept in his wallet a poem by Pasolini, who also came to such a violent end! And Valeria, who was half-knowingly sacrificing herself in the hope of having Michael's assassin arrested. And he, Luigi, who went along and played dirty, hoping to find personal redemption by solving a case without fear of criticism, of marginalization, of death; all in the hope of leaving 1991 behind, of setting himself free from his heinous past. Luigi Sasta was not sleepy; the afternoon nap had given him a boost of vitality. He flipped open the cellphone, his only companion of these past few years, and crossed over to the other side of the street, seeking a quiet place next to the pizzeria.

"Hello ..."

"Elena?"

"*Papà*, do you know how late it is?"

"I'm sorry, I just wanted to tell you what a lovely time I had the other night. It's been a long time since we shared an evening like that ..."

"So true ...how's the case going?"

Luigi started walking again, the phone glued to his ear, while crowds parted to let him through.

"It's been a hard day, but I have come across some important elements and would love to talk to you about them."

"Tonight?"

"Whenever you like."

"Well, I was writing, but I am bored out of my mind. Come over!"

"I'll go get the car. I'll be there shortly."

"I'm here, but you must promise me something ..."

"What?"

"That you won't smoke. You did not look well last night."

"I was just tired. I'll be there soon."

Luigi flipped the phone shut and walked along Clinton Street. The brightly lit-up patio of one of the restaurants, with the toing and froing of the waiters and the clamour on the tables reminded him of famous scenes of Roman nightlife in films from the sixties. Wouldn't it be wonderful to close the street to the traffic so all these people could eat *alfresco*, Luigi thought as he turned into an alleyway towards his garage. Before opening the doors to the garage he stopped to look at the moon playing hide-and-seek among clouds floating freely over the steeple of St. Francis's Church. He would not like to die on such a night. He had so much he wanted to share with

Elena; he wanted to talk about his dreams, about his return to Italy, about the case and maybe even about his health. He wanted to wait for her in a house in the country, a house on the hills he wanted to buy, near Fermo, in the Marches region; an area where plums were left unharvested and white wine flowed like water. His reverie was interrupted by the promise he had made to Elena, so he lit up a du Maurier in order to forestall a withdrawal crisis. He glanced again at the moon, listening to the muted sounds coming from the main street. It occurred to him that Michael Karrier's past and his own were bound together, half-asleep, on that corner just behind the road, invisible, suffocating and alive. He decided to get his Subaru and make a pit stop at Bar Italia to get some ice cream. He had forgotten Elena's favourite flavour so he would buy a mix of coffee, *bacio perugina* and lemon.

When he opened the garage door Luigi looked at the Subaru in what he thought was the gloomy light of the moon, until he remembered that the light came from a lamppost in the alley, the same light that crept irritatingly into his bedroom. Luigi was slave to an old habit, one of many he had brought over from Italy: he preferred sleeping in the dark, in total darkness, at night as well as during the afternoon nap that he allowed himself on Sundays. Preparing for sleep had become a nightly ritual. In a series of gestures resembling a religious ceremony Luigi removed his day clothes and put on pyjamas that had been freshly laundered. He took pride in his collection of pyjamas, silk for summer and striped flannel for winter. When he pulled open the drawers and saw them all neatly laid out, seductively fragrant, he was overcome with an unexpected and giddy sense of well-being.

There were times when he neglected his appearance: he could wear the same shirt for a couple of days, loosely knotted ties that had seen better days, wrinkled worn-out raincoats, an unbecoming five-o'clock shadow, but he never neglected his pyjamas. They were his refuge.

Luigi turned to look at his rusty old Subaru and got behind the driver's seat. He turned the ignition key, but the engine gave no signs of life. Only then did it occur to him that he had run out of gas, or at least he hoped this was the reason. He left the garage and whistled his way to College Street, looking for a taxi, hoping to find a newly landed driver to whom he could call out directions, empathizing with his need for understanding. And when the driver would ask him where he came from, he might reply that he was Italian, or maybe he would lie to avoid being stereotyped as Italian/Mafia.

The investigative team excludes any Mafia-type settling of scores.
NEW DEVELOPMENTS IN THE MURDER AT THE ART GALLERY
By Luigi Sasta

According to our latest information, the investigative team has established the weapon used to kill Michele Carrieri, the Italian found dead two days ago at the Art Gallery of Ontario. The murder weapon is a "puntillo" or "puntilla," a type of stiletto dagger with a long, wide blade used in bullfights to finish off the bull once he has fallen on his knees after the bullfighter has struck him. In a thorough police questioning, Carrieri's live-in partner denied any connection between the victim and Mafia or criminal elements. The team's investigation, following an exchange of research with their Italian counterparts, lends support to her claims.

According to the coroner's initial report, a decisive "puntillo" stabbing to the cerebellum resulted in the immediate death of the victim, entering the back of the neck at the nape, cutting through the carotid on the left side and the subclavian artery.

The autopsy will be completed within a few hours, and the findings will be released to the investigative team within a day or two. Apparently, though, the likely identification of the murder weapon complicates the investigation. Should the findings confirm that the murder weapon was a "puntillo," the investigators are faced with a signature killing that is completely new to Toronto, and that points to a killer who is skilled in the use of this type of weapon. And, although the police have not leaked anything on the matter, it is clear that while this narrows the gap on the investigation, it also opens up new possible scenarios. So, while the dynamics of Michele Carrieri's killing appear clear enough, the motive remains clouded in mystery. The Italian consulate in Toronto sent a note of condolences to the family and friends of the victim. A funeral service will be announced in the next few days.

T*he mystery of Michele Carrieri's death*
DIGGING INTO MICHELE CARRIERI'S PAST
By Luigi Sasta

The murder of Michele Carrieri two days ago at the Art Gallery of Ontario raises troubling questions on his background. The victim was an Italian who came to Canada twelve years ago and who had changed his name to Michael Karrier.

Why does an Italian, an immigrant, decide to move to Canada and change his name? Why would a man who, by all accounts of friends and family, lived a normal life, meet with such a cruel death? Setting aside for lack of any evidence – as the investigators themselves have done – the theory of a Mafia-style settling of accounts and, given Karrier's secluded lifestyle, the motive of a crime of passion, what was there in his past or his future that cut his life so short while still so young?

These are some of the questions we, and the investigators, are seeking to answer.

As he did every day, Michele Carrieri left his office for lunch and walked over to the Gallery to see an exhibit, entered into a screening room and there, under cover of darkness, was stabbed to death.

We now know that the murder weapon may have been a "puntillo," a short knife, a type of dagger used to finish off the bull in the throes of death following the matador's sword thrust.

What symbols lurk behind this bloody murder? An old enemy's revenge? A ritual understood only by an inner circle and delivered through the use of the puntillo?

The weapon of choice is part and parcel of a sophisticated and cruel ritual like a bullfight. If we suppose that in the past Michele Carrieri might have been part of a secret society and consider the specific weapon used in his murder, and the act of the killing itself, we can conclude that the victim was killed for one of two reasons: one, he was intent on leaving the sect; or two, he was a traitor.

So far, we know little if anything, and the investigators themselves have no clue as to the motive.

Let's leave this line of reasoning and follow another path: the murderer's. Who might be able to use the puntillo with enough skill and precision to kill a man in his prime?

We know through our reading that the puntilla, "the act itself of delivering the deadly blow," is usually practiced by one of the men who helps the matador, and in some cases by skilled butchers. In any case, be it at the hands of the matador's helper or of an ordinary butcher, the act of delivering the single final mortal blow to the bull is part of a ritual requiring a mastery that leaves no room for improvisation. That is how we feel about all this.

Chapter 11
June 7

On reading the article, Luigi was not very happy with himself. Had he made the right decision in failing to mention the newspaper clipping found in Karrier's wallet? Or his ties of friendship with Santamaria, whose photo appeared in the story? Or the vanished picture mentioned by Valeria? Or yesterday's attack by the Peruvian? Why had he not cited the name of the Peruvian and the friendship between Michele Carrieri and the politician Santamaria?

These questions continued to plague Luigi even after he sat down at his desk at *Stampa Italica* after having put out a small fire of protest, started by Arazzi, over the air conditioning.

Luigi was not in the habit of shutting down protests, especially when they were justified, as it was impossible to work in the torrid heat. He was well-aware of this, in view of his health. Every morning he would wake up in the vain hope that a rainfall might clear the muggy air, but the sun continued to beat down mercilessly. Yet he had been successful, one more time, in getting everyone back to their desks, promising to talk with the publisher who was due to arrive shortly, flashing the sparkling smile and garish bowtie that drove everyone beyond the pale. In his little speech to the staff he had appealed to their sense of social responsibility in the community, to their journalistic mission, to the historic role of *Stampa Italica*. The speech had been met with approval; even Arazzi had liked it and quietened down; finally Luigi could go back to reading his copy of *Stampa Italica*.

He shut the door to his office, flung open the window, plugged in a portable fan which he placed on his desk and spread open his copy of *Stampa Italica*. Yesterday's failed attack had stopped him from stating all he knew, most of which he had pieced together from Valeria's accounts. He feared for her, for her life, and he wanted to spare her unnecessary pain should he tarnish her memory of Michael Karrier. This was why he had not liked his articles even though his colleagues, not to speak of *Signorina* Arianna, sang his praises. Most of all he regretted keeping from the public the fact that Valeria had become the bait with which to catch the murderer. He thought back with a great deal of distress to Elena's accusations who, in spite of the recent thaw in their relationship she never failed to throw in his face his indecisiveness on that bad business in 1991 and his shamelessly vaunted objectivity.

What had happened to the famous "coolness" of which he was so proud, the surgical detachment of the investigator whose only goal is the final result? To top it all off, even his Subaru had refused to budge, and a neighbour who worked as a mechanic had declared it ready for the junkyard, a predicament that distressed Luigi greatly. He put aside thoughts of his Subaru and returned to his reading of *Stampa Italica*. He was not pleased. He left his desk and moved to the window, letting his gaze loose on the cars that were crowding the highway exit. The morning light was violent, the sky clear. In spite of it all Luigi was feeling well; his angina was leaving him in peace for a while. The doctor had warned him to avoid unnecessary exertion, to rest, especially in this heat, and, "above all ...!"? Above all he had to stop smoking or face one of two possible outcomes: death or surgical intervention.

Luigi did not shiver, though he was overcome with a strange feeling, a clenching in his stomach and his chest, a sudden urge to resolve this case, to set everything in order before his possible departure. He wanted to regain Elena's trust, her respect; he wanted to help Valeria, to get to the truth, to bring justice to bear. He turned towards his desk and saw the package of du Mauriers and the lighter resting next to each other like lifelong friends, his only friends. He would solve the case and the very next day he would leave for Italy, but to where?

For years he had nursed the idea of a return, of buying a small farm in Petritoli in the Marches and devoting his remaining years to writing. Maybe it was high time he retired ... but he did not want to leave on the sly, he must leave some sign of his passage in the country in which he had lived for so many years. Now that he was alone Luigi no longer understood the reasons for living in a place where he had never really felt at home, mostly because of the language, his accented English.

He sympathized with Michael Karrier, who must have come here to follow a dream only to wake up in a nightmare. Many before him, forced to leave home in search of work, had followed the same pipe dream, and how many of them had come here hoping to put behind them a difficult, inconvenient past? Karrier probably believed he could smother his remorse by diving into a new life from which he could surface a new, honest man. Even Luigi's own family found themselves, one fine day, in a strange country forced to carve out a new life. Even though the conditions had been very different, Luigi was overcome with a fellow feeling for the young victim. Whatever the circumstances, it takes courage to run away.

But in spite of all his theories Luigi felt there was something else uniting them; perhaps his meeting with Valeria, or the poem in the wallet, something he could not quite put his finger on, something he felt but could not explain. He moved back to his desk, picked up the receiver and dialed Valeria's number.

"Yes?"

"*Buon giorno*, Valeria. It's me, Sasta. How are you?"

There was no reply from Valeria Furlon. Luigi reached for his package of du Mauriers and lit one up nervously.

"I called you to see if we could meet."

"Why?"

"Because only you and I can resolve this case and save Michael's name from being dragged in the mud ..."

"I don't think we can do much."

Luigi and Valeria were quiet for a moment or two, then Valeria continued. "I am on my way to the university. I can't stand it here; I think I am going crazy. Let's meet there."

"Where?"

"On the campus, in front of Cucchi's water sculpture."

"How about in three hours?"

"OK."

Valeria hung up before Luigi could warn her to be careful. He stood there a while, cigarette in one hand and the receiver in the other, before putting out the cigarette and hanging up.

On the gaudy dial of the horrible clock on the wall, the soccer player's leg kicked the football every passing second. Luigi got up from his desk, stood on a chair, yanked the clock from the wall and threw it in the trashcan. He returned to his desk, changed his mind, picked up the clock, left his office and headed to the newsroom, asking in a loud voice if anyone wanted the clock. They all raised their hands, but Arazzi was quick to grab it.

Luigi approached *Signorina* Arianna, who seemed displeased, and reassured her: "Don't worry, *Signorina*, I'll get you another gift ..."

She looked at him; her sad eyes sparkled with a single flash of joy.

"Thank you, *Dottore*, but please don't worry about me."

Luigi, feeling regretful, sensed a rising nausea in his stomach.

… BETWEEN ROTHKO AND 3 WINDOWS

Chapter 12

Luigi had not been on a bus for many years, but since his Subaru had given up the ghost, he travelled by public transport and came into contact with a whole new world. A crowd of humans he had never noticed, sleepy, silent, frightened, exhausted. Not that he was unaware of it, but up to now he had only observed it in fragments, in offices, banks, stores. All you had to do was take a bus to the suburbs or the subway in rush hour to see the fragments of this disparate humanity congeal into a mass like drops of mercury in a test tube.

The bus ride to the university provided enough clues to understand the new population, the new citizens of Toronto. At each stop men, women and children of different races climbed on and off; former Afghani soldiers, former warriors from Somalia, former Russians, former Yugoslavians, former citizens of Hong Kong, former Vietcong, former partisans, former torturers, former gentlemen, former peasants, former … former … former … mercury shrapnel blown from closed factories, floods, ethnic conflicts, religious wars, fallen walls, triumphs of the free market, the fall of ideologies … drops of mercury splattered on refugee wagons, barges, trucks, rescue planes, helicopters … all of them aiming to congeal in Toronto.

In the midst of this cacophony of voices and sounds coming from so far away, Luigi was forging a new relationship with his city, moved by the shy curiosity and the uneasy feeling of someone who has been invited to a party where he knows no one. The faceless humanity that crowded the subway cars and the sweaty buses did not read *Stampa Italica*. Luigi thought there could be no better city in which to erase the past, or to believe that the past could be erased. Like his colleagues and his clownish publisher, was Luigi not simply a foreigner desperately clinging to a life raft of a language and traditions still barely afloat in this new, stormy sea? And for how long? Ghosts from the past, as Elena said.

What was the point in struggling against these waves? Was it not better to let go, to float downstream, till you ran out of strength? To offer no resistance and to disappear by merging, like water flowing into water, into this new protective society, to assimilate by forgetting the past and entering into a silent future, deaf to the roar coming from Kabul, from Sarajevo, from Mogadishu ...

"Michael referred to them as prick heads ..."

Luigi turned and saw Valeria taking her leave from a student to whom she handed over a couple of manila file folders, then he shifted his gaze to the plaintive obelisks of the Cucchi sculpture at the entrance to the university. When he looked back he noticed the student scurrying off in a hurry. He was momentarily distracted by Valeria's remarks as she approached him.

"When the artist came to Toronto he said that he had wanted to create a typical Italian piazza, a meeting place where students could come together in dialogue; he referred to it as an act of civic reform ..."

"How are you, Valeria?" Luigi asked, paying little attention to her remarks on Cucchi and his obelisks, though he did share Michael Karrier's impression on the phallic appearance of the obelisks.

"I read your articles. Looks like you are getting close to something that could turn out to be true," Valeria said.

"Why do you think that?"

"Because when I read your pieces I became aware that Michael was hiding something from his life ..."

"You never knew? How is it possible that you could not see through to it? I must ask this, Valeria, please don't be angry ..."

"Go on ..."

"Let's set aside a narrative of jealousy and –"

"Cheating." Valeria struggled to hold back her tears. "I don't know. Why don't you tell me ..."

Valeria looked over at the statues and smiled.

"Let's set that aside," Luigi repeated, "and let's also exclude a Mafia-style killing. It's clear that Michele was killed for something he must have done in his past life."

"How can you be so sure?"

"Listen ... today, riding on the bus, I finally understood that there aren't many places in the world, I mean, places where you can not only hide, but erase yourself and your past in the hope of building a new life, as you can here in Canada. This is a country built on the future, on the crossing out of the past, like plastic surgery on identity."

"So, according to you, Michele came here to trade in his face, to change his identity." Valeria glowered at him.

"Yes, on this I have no doubts, even though I might have chosen a new name that was not so similar to the original: it's as though Michael did not really want to completely wipe out Michele," Luigi replied, as he gently took Valeria by the arm, guiding her towards the campus.

"According to the police, Michele had been part of one of those leftist student movements in the seventies," Luigi said as they walked along the campus, with Valeria following him in silence, "and I would not be surprised to discover that all his friends in the picture were militants in the same group, including Raul Santamaria, who is today a leader of the separatist party."

"Go on."

"I am not sure I can picture in my mind what may have taken place between Michele and Santamaria, what they may have done together, something illegal, something terrible from which Michele could hide no longer, something over which he did not expect to feel remorse but then wanted to return to Italy, to confess everything ..."

Valeria came to a sudden stop. "What everything?"

"Only you can tell me."

"But I don't know anything," she protested in a loud voice, attracting the attention of a student who was approaching them.

"Listen to me, Valeria: Michele was butchered in a cruel way, and we could have been killed too, were it not for your *sang-froid*. Our situation, in case you haven't figured it out, is extremely dangerous."

"What proofs do you have, *Signor* Sasta?"

"None, other than a newspaper clipping in a wallet, a murder at the Art Gallery, and a Latino who wanted to kill us. Don't you understand, Valeria, I fear for your life," Luigi said, looking mournfully at her.

"Michele was the best man I ever met."

Luigi's intense gaze did not waver even as he fumbled in his coat pocket for his cigarettes.

"The man you knew was another Michele, he was Michael Karrier." They stood facing each other in silence.

"I want to help you, but I can only do so if I can uncover Michele's past, his true past, the past that not even you knew about or imagined. Michael wanted to lay his cards on the table, and that's why he was killed."

Valeria turned away from him.

"I cannot help you, I don't know how to help you," she said and dashed towards the entrance to the university.

Luigi Sasta watched as Valeria Furlon disappeared beyond the main portal of the institute, and only then did he notice the student to whom Valeria had handed the manila envelope. He was lurking behind the window of a fast-food shop on the other side of the campus, but Luigi had recognized him on the spot. He tried to approach him, but the student was already on the run. Luigi trundled back towards the statues and lit up a cigarette. "At least these prick heads are good for something," he thought, heading for a shady spot for protection from the sun.

Chapter 13
June 11

A few days went by and the Italian team started playing in the World Cup. On College Street and on St. Clair, Toronto's two Little Italys (though in fact there were many Little Italys in Toronto, with the biggest one in the suburbs), Italian fans crowded the bars and cafés, making fun of the Portuguese, who had not even qualified for the Cup and so gave their support to the Brazilian team. The Italians found this unacceptable, considered it a betrayal.

Over at *Stampa Italica*, they were scraping the bottom of the news barrel and settled on making predictions about the outcome of the World Cup, while in the newsroom they carried on with the usual squabbles. In the relentless heat Luigi felt weaker by the day and increasingly frustrated with his failure to make any progress in the Karrier murder case. Although Sergeant Stevens called frequently enough, he had nothing of any substance for him. Lucio Marros had vanished. His phone calls to Valeria went unanswered, and Elena accepted his dinner invitations but with little enthusiasm. Luigi had just returned to his office at *Stampa Italica* from the Miracca Funeral Home where Michael Karrier had been cremated. Only Valeria, Luigi, a colleague or two of Michael's, the Vice-Consul and his driver were present at the ceremony. Luigi was at a loss as to why he had shown up, out of respect for Valeria or to find God knows what. After a quick handshake with the Vice-Consul and his driver, Valeria did not wish to stay longer and headed outside to the waiting limousine carrying Michael Karrier's coffin.

She had made a sign to Luigi, who looked at her in silence. He remembered Michael Karrier's wish and thought that Valeria might be going to spread his ashes on Lake Ontario in the vicinity of the R.C. Harris Water Filtration Plant.

Luigi's back now ached, on his left side at the height of the shoulder blade, and he found it difficult to breathe. Journalists came into his office with half-baked ideas for stories without any meat, carrying on their litany of complaints about the heat and the air conditioning.

Fed up with it all, he finally got up from his desk, locked the door to his office and walked back to pick up the telephone. He called the Italian telephone directory assistance office, asking for the number of Santamaria's political party. He looked at the telephone for the longest time before dialing the number. He lit up a du Maurier and waited.

"Independent Party, good evening ..."

"Good evening. My name is Luigi Sasta, and I am the editor-in-chief of *Stampa Italica*, the Italian language daily in Canada. I am calling from Toronto and would like to speak with *Dottore* Santamaria ..."

"Wait a moment."

"Yes. Could you please tell him I would like an interview? What's the weather like over there?"

"It's unbearably hot. Lucky you, to be in the cold ..."

"Not really, we are suffering through a dreadful heat wave."

"Oh, I did not realize that it could get so hot in Canada. Wait a moment."

Luigi looked at the cigarette burning out between his fingers, felt the rapid heartbeats in his chest and wondered whether he was doing the right thing. What would he ask Santamaria?

"Are you still there?"

"Yes, I am on the line."

"Good, I'll transfer you to the honourable member Santamaria."

"Thank you."

"Hello?"

"*Dottore* Santamaria?"

"Yes, it's me. To whom do I have the pleasure of speaking?"

"I am Luigi Sasta, the editor-in-chief of *Stampa Italica*, the Italian language daily in Canada."

"Ah yes, I think I may have read your paper. It's a pleasure to know that our compatriots read the news in Italian. How can I help you?"

"I have some questions for you."

"Good, ask away. By the way, is it snowing at your end?"

"No, *onorevole*, it's unbearably hot."

"Good."

"*Onorevole*, were you ever acquainted with a certain Michele Carrieri?" As he asked the question Luigi felt something like an explosion in his brain, his chest and his lungs. But he stayed cool.

"Excuse me?" Raul Santamaria asked after a long pause.

"*Onorevole*, did you know Michele Carrieri?"

"Excuse me, but why are you asking me this?"

"Because Michele Carrieri, who had changed his name to Michael Karrier here in Canada, was murdered last week, killed with a knife."

"Should I know him?"

"I don't know, that is why I am calling you. We found a newspaper clipping in his wallet, an article with your picture in it."

"Yes, he was a schoolmate, many years ago. He was killed? I'm sorry to hear that."

"How many years since you last saw him?"

"As I told you, he was a schoolmate, so it's been quite a few years … but, excuse me, just because you find an article on me in his wallet you feel obliged to call me?"

"You must forgive me, but the police are in the dark, and there are no clues. I thought you might help us reconstruct Carrieri's life."

"Listen to me. I have nothing to add to what I have already told you. What did you say your name was?"

"Luigi Sasta from *Stampa Italica*. So, *onorevole*, you say you have never seen Carrieri since your school years? But forgive me one last question. Were you ever in Peru with Michele Carrieri?"

"You've got some nerve. Yes ... yes, but I have no intention to answer any more of your questions."

"Does the name Lucio Marros mean anything to you?"

Raul Santamaria hung up.

Luigi paused with the receiver in his hand before gently putting it down. How could he have been so stupid as to put his cards on the table? It was clear Santamaria was holding back on the truth and had left Luigi with the impression that his questions had completely unhinged him. He got up to unlock the door, then made his way back to his desk to write a quick article for the front page. He dialed *Signorina* Arianna, who picked up immediately.

"*Signorina* ..."

"Yes?"

"I am going home."

"Are you not feeling well, *Dottore*?"

"No, yes, I don't know ... Listen, today there will most likely be calls from the publisher and the Ambassador. Tell them that I am away at some meetings and that I will be back tomorrow. I have written a piece for the front page to go with the story on the conflict between the police and First Nations People. I leave the rest to you, business as usual ... OK?"

"Yes, *Dottore*. Anything else?"

"Yes, kindly call me a taxi, and please don't call me at home unless it's something of the utmost importance. If someone is in a hurry to speak with me, please get their number and tell them I'll call back this evening."

"Will do, *Dottore*."

"Should Sergeant Stevens call, tell him I'll call back. Understood?"

"Is there anything else, *Dottore*?"

Luigi hung up, retrieved his jacket and made his way slowly down the stairs. By now he was very familiar with the attacks. He knew the fear and was gripped by the terror of death along with all the usual symptoms that seemed to flare up from their sleep like an eruption. Luigi saw the taxi arrive just behind the truck returning with the unsold papers. He swallowed his first nitroglycerin pill.

Funeral services held yesterday for the victim at the Art Gallery
KARRIER OR CARRIERI, DYING FAR FROM HOME
By Luigi Sasta

Only a handful of people were in attendance at the Miracca Funeral Home. He died far away from home, murdered in a barbaric way in a famous gallery in the city. Originally Italian, he died a naturalized Canadian citizen. One week after the murder the detectives have yet to discover any useful leads in the investigation.

All we know of Michele Carrieri is that he was born in Milan and that as a young student he had belonged to organized leftist protest movements and that when he moved to Canada he anglicised his name and surname to Michael Karrier. Here he met a woman, and the two of them apparently lived an uneventful life together.

Soon after the discovery of the murder weapon the investigation stalled and seems to have reached a dead end. Prior to being murdered, Michael Karrier lived a normal life, perhaps *too normal. That is why the investigation must look to his past, focusing on events that took place long ago and far away from Canada. How else to explain that none of his old friends, assuming that he had any, came forward? How likely is it that, once he landed in Canada, he could wipe out his past and reach that state of anonymity he craved by simply changing his name and surname?*

Yesterday morning at the funeral for Michele Carrieri, only his life partner, one or two colleagues and some consular representatives were present. When facing death we all wonder what our legacy will be. It's a question we also ask about Michele Carrieri. What did he leave behind?

Surely there must have been friends and family in Italy, where the victim spent most of his life, who might have wished to pay their respects? Or is it likely that no relative or friend came to Canada out of fear?

It seems impossible to think that today there are Italians who still immigrate to Canada, yet Michele Carrieri was just such an immigrant.

It is for this reason that we have decided to reveal a detail we discovered immediately after the murder, something we had held back in order not to derail the investigation. We reveal this detail today because, in our view, it is relevant: in his wallet Carrieri kept a newspaper clipping of an interview, with a picture, of an Italian politician, someone who had been a boyhood friend. We now believe that the article is a key element in the solution of the murder case.

Carrieri had no siblings and his parents had died long ago, which made his decision to sever all links with his past by moving to Canada easier. We continue to ask ourselves who Carrieri or Karrier might have been, but the answer remains elusive.

Chapter 14

Luigi returned home. He undressed in his usual meticulous manner, pulled down the blinds and lay down on the bed. Waves of cool air coming from the air conditioner made it easier for him to breathe. His aches and pains had vanished after the first nitroglycerin pill, but an exhaustion had set in that was so debilitating that he couldn't follow a coherent thought. The urge to smoke never left him. Tonight he might call Sergeant Stevens to tell him about the telephone call to Santamaria, knowing he would end up listening patiently to his protestations and advice. Now the only thing that mattered was to close his eyes and fall asleep. Luigi thought back to his phone call a few hours ago with Santamaria, trying to find some clarity by focusing on the tone of the conversation. It was pretty clear that there had been some *omertà* on Santamaria's part, but to jump to the conclusion that this implied a link to Carrieri's murder was a stretch, to say the least. He would need some proof on the extent of their involvement, but he knew that he was on the right track, was certain that Santamaria knew a lot more than he had said, that he had played a part in Michele's past, a past that had sealed his fate. Luigi struggled out of bed, went into the living room and dialed Sergeant Stevens's number.

"*Ciao*, it's Sasta."
"Any news?"
"Maybe. Any news on the Latino?"
"No."
"Nothing at all?"
"Nothing."

"I spoke with Santamaria ..."

"When?"

"Two, maybe three hours ago?"

"What did he tell you?"

"At first he was noncommittal, then he admitted knowing him. We did not speak for long, but I am convinced he knows a lot more than he is willing to share."

"That was a risky move."

"I know." Luigi paused, then continued, "But if we don't force the situation we risk getting nowhere ..."

"You sound tired."

"I am tired, Stevens, but I don't want to let this case go. I am sure the Latino is the key to everything. If you can get to him you'll have it solved!"

"How can you be so sure?"

"I just know it! But I called you for another reason ... I am afraid that something might happen to Valeria Furlon. You should keep an eye on her."

"I'll do what I can."

"Meaning?"

"Meaning I can't have my men act as her babysitters."

"What do you mean you won't act as her babysitter? She's the one at risk here, more than anyone else. Are you giving up on the case?"

"What the hell ..."

"I get it, it's just like the last time."

"Which last time?"

"I'll call you in a few days. "

Luigi hung up. He felt his heart beat faster, felt the pain returning to his neck and shoulders, arriving from faraway and taking a run up for the long jump. He dialed Valeria's home number, but there was no answer. He tried the university, but they told him Valeria had no classes that day. In frustration he called *Stampa Italica*.

"*Stampa Italica*, good morning."
"Good morning, Arazzi. It's me, Sasta."
"Ah good morning, *Dottore*. Have you heard?"
"No."
"The Italian team has tied the game, but don't worry. We'll get into the semi-finals, no problem."
"Arazzi, I am not worried in the least."
"I was just saying, *Dottore* ... So why don't you like soccer?"
"Arazzi, is *Signorina* Arianna there?"
"I'll get her, right away." Arazzi's tone gave him away; he was so heartbroken to work for an editor who had so little passion for the game.
"Good morning, *Dottore*."
"Good morning. Please listen, *Signorina*. Should *Signora* Furlon call, please tell her to call me at home immediately."
"Of course, *Dottore*. You should know that since you left the phone has not stopped ringing, just as you said: the Ambassador, the usual crop of parliamentarians, the publisher. They are all looking for you, they all want to talk to you."
"Santamaria's power ..."
"What did you say?"
"Nothing. I am not available for anyone, except *Signora* Furlon. Please tell her I am at home!"
"Your daughter called."
"Yes. Good. Thank you. Please review the front page and drop my piece to below the fold, understood?"
"Yes, *Dottore*, thank you, please have some rest."
"Thank you, *Signorina*."

Luigi hung up and made his way back to the bedroom. He took another pill from his coat pocket, went into the bathroom, turned on the tap and drank a sip of water. He returned to the bedroom, opened the chest of drawers under the armoire, removed a cardboard box and placed it on the bed.

His chest was exploding, his head was spinning, but Luigi untied the string that held together the box and rummaged through the contents until he found a yellow envelope. He opened it and took out a document. It was his last will and testament. He looked at it, read it and lay down on the bed, placing the document on his chest. Luigi waited for the pill to kick in. On the bedside table there were other pills; he had two more chances before rushing off to emergency. He took another pill and thought of the soccer game. In his mind's eye he saw the referee admonishing him: another foul and you're out, another pill ...

Chapter 15

Signorina Arianna had called him that afternoon to let him know that many television stations and dailies in the city, and a reporter from a famous newspaper in Italy, had bombarded the newsroom of *Stampa Italica* looking for updates and clarifications on the case. He decided to speak to no one, preferring to wait for a move from Santamaria. Not to mention the many phone calls by the Ambassador, added *Signorina* Arianna, who finally lost his patience and took it out on her, or the angry calls from the publisher.

Clearly Santamaria had friends in high places, Luigi thought. As if there could be any doubt; he smiled, put down the phone, turned off the ringer and lay down on the bed.

He was able to sleep for a few hours but woke up in the middle of the night feeling even more tired. Tomorrow he would call Elena and tell her about his angina. Pages from his will had slid down from the bed onto the floor. He glanced at them, thinking that he had often felt very weak after an angina attack, but tonight he was overcome by something else, a sense of nausea and disgust with his life at the paper. He should leave *Stampa Italica*, once and for all, and move to Petritoli, that village on the hills in the Marches near Fermo where fava beans are plentiful and white wine flows freely. Maybe he was just too old or maybe it was his angina, but Luigi just did not have it in him to go on with all his personal struggles.

He thought back to the dreary funeral service for Carrieri and to his meeting with Valeria, who seemed eager to avoid him. He was still afraid for her. He moved to the living room and turned on the television. Many of the channels carried the World Cup games, and Italy, in spite of having tied this game, was still considered by the experts, along with a couple of other teams, as a favourite to win. He turned off the set and once again dialed *Signorina* Arianna's number, who, given the hour, was at home. He instructed her to fax a copy of his article on the case to the headquarters of Santamaria's political party and to follow up by sending via courier all of the *Stampa Italica* editions that dealt with the Carrieri case. She was also to set up an appointment with Santamaria in Milan for next week. He would pay for the flight. This might be his last case, and Luigi did not wish to leave any stone unturned. He was sure Santamaria would see him, but should he refuse, Luigi was ready to force the issue and expose him. At this point, who gave a shit about any potential fallout? It was high time he retired ...

He went back to bed, overcome by an unspeakable exhaustion. He felt another attack coming on and took one more nitroglycerin pill. Goddamned angina! He lay down and waited for the usual symptoms to materialize out of the darkness, to advance towards him like spiders or rats coming from some crack in the walls. Finally he fell asleep. But not before he came to the conclusion that he had reached the point of no return, that there were some loose ends he should attend to, especially with Elena.

Chapter 16

Luigi was too weak to respond; too weak to even try getting up off the bed from which he looked on as his worried daughter listened to his family doctor's complaints, accusing his patient of a lack of cooperation.

Elena nodded in approval at the doctor's warnings, who, having examined Luigi, shook his head repeatedly as if to say that he was casting his words to the wind. He made one last half-hearted attempt and ordered the patient to never again go near a cigarette.

"In any case, regardless of your smoking, you have to surrender to the evidence, you can no longer postpone the operation; a neat bypass and you'll feel much better. But keep in mind that unless you make some changes in your way of life, and above all quit smoking altogether, your recovery will be compromised." Elena looked at her father imploringly, but Luigi was busy devising ways to be free of both of them so he could light up.

"*Papà*, do you understand? No more macho attitudes ..."

"Yes ... yes ... OK, I'll try to quit smoking. Doctor, tell me more about this operation ..."

The doctor looked at Luigi in disbelief, fixing his gaze on him.

"If you are really serious about it – and you must be because your angina won't allow you not to be – and if you are serious about a change in your way of life ..."

The doctor paused, raising his index finger in the air, which Luigi found very irritating but was too tired to engage in a rebuttal. And in any case the doctor was also an old friend who was only trying to help him.

"I will send you to a specialist, a friend of mine, and will book a time in the hospital ..."

"What are my chances of a positive result?" Luigi asked.

"Excellent, but, as I told you, a lot depends on the patient's cooperation."

Luigi felt Elena observing him closely, and he tried to avoid her gaze.

"All right, Doctor. I'm in your hands."

Elena saw the doctor out. Luigi heard the two of them talking on the street before Elena returned to the bedroom.

"So, how long do I have?" Luigi asked.

"This is not the time to joke around, *Papà*." Elena sat on the edge of the bed.

"I am not joking, Elena. I want to know the truth!"

"No more, no less than what the doctor told you, *Papà*. You must look after yourself, maybe stop working ..."

"Working at ... what did you call it?"

"I don't remember ..."

"Don't lie to me, Elena!"

"If anyone is lying here it's you, going so far as to keep me in the dark about your angina ... I must leave now, I have to go to the university. I'll stay here for a few days, what do you think?" Elena stood up and turned away from him.

"I'm not dead yet, you know. But just in case, I looked over my will, and you are my only heir."

"Thanks, *Papà*. Let's talk about that some other time."

Luigi Sasta did not feel like continuing, especially on noticing that Elena's eyes were clear, which gave him no pleasure.

"What's the weather like?" he asked.

Elena did not reply.

"Is it still hot?"

With her finger Elena lifted a slat in the blinds and

looked out the window. "It's still humid and threatening to rain," she said.

"Can I look, too?" Valeria raised the blinds. Luigi moved his gaze over the roofs of neighbouring houses overlooking his backyard.

"I've had little time for the garden this year," he said in a feeble voice.

"You never did have time for the garden, *Papà*!" Elena reminded him.

Luigi nodded in agreement, saying, "Well, I did plant a flower now and then ..."

"They were dead within a few days, as you never watered them; it was always Mother who looked after the garden. Look at it now, just a wild patch."

"So it is ..."

"I am going, *Papà*."

"Yes. Go on. Thanks again for coming over."

"You don't need to thank me, *Papà!*"

"Elena?"

"Yes?" Elena stopped on the threshold to the bedroom and turned to face him. She was apprehensive.

"You are not obliged to come here, you know."

"I know."

"But if you want to keep coming, I am pleased. We could discuss the Carrieri case ..."

"Carrieri is dead, *Papà*, and you are alive," she retorted, with irritation, and left the room.

Luigi heard his daughter lock the front door and, looking out the window, he tried to fall asleep, in vain. Memories of Elena as a child jumping naked on the bed in which he lay while Mariuccia attempted to dress her; the grief-stricken face of Valeria Furlon, the grimace of Michele Carrieri; Sergeant Stevens's racist jokes; the predatory gaze of Lucio Marros, all those articles for *Stampa Italica*: a carousel of thoughts and memories crowded his brain and pressed against the inside of his head, triggering a great, primordial fatigue. Luigi looked at the darkening sky and closed his eyes. What time was it? He turned towards the night table; an old clock he had bought with Mariuccia reminded him it was four in the afternoon.

This was just about the saddest, strangest case he had come across in his long career. There had been many others, some desolate, some squalid, others violent, but never anything as sad as Michele Carrieri's attempts to change his life by coming to Canada. Luigi could see his efforts at integration, could intuit his suffering and remorse, as there could be no doubt that Carrieri must have done something really big in the past, something he came to regret. Luigi felt he was walking in the victim's tentative footsteps, which seemed to grow firmer with every passing day. Michael Karrier became slowly accustomed to life in Canada and soon fell in love with Valeria. But his serenity was constantly disturbed by memories, by remorse, and perhaps also by his decision to return to Italy to finally spill the beans. And just when he was ready to take this leap, he was murdered. How many times had he read the poem he kept in his wallet, how many times had he lingered over those words, thinking about the curse of loneliness that hung over the life his mother gave him?

Luigi dozed off, floating into a delirium of pleasure at the memory of a du Maurier at the racetrack, many years ago, when he handed over baby Elena into Mariuccia's arms to spare her the second-hand smoke, to avoid poisoning her with the same cigarette that blocked his heart.

Luigi slept for a long time. Late in the evening the phone awakened him. Groggy with tiredness, he reached for his phone.

"Hello?"

"We have met before," a man's voice replied, speaking Italian with a strong Spanish accent.

In spite of his exhaustion, Luigi understood immediately; his heart went into overdrive.

"At the R.C. Harris Water Filtration Plant?"

"Not exactly. We saw each other at a café on Queen Street. At the water filtration plant I would have loved to make your acquaintance, but you called your friends."

"What do you want?"

"I want to meet with you, tonight at 11 in the Convento Rico club, not too far from where you live. You have something that belongs to me. I want it back, and I don't want to see any of your friends buzzing about."

"What?"

"It's a photograph. I want it back tonight!"

"Why should I come?"

"So you can spare Valeria Furlon unnecessary suffering."

"Where is Valeria?" Luigi asked, but the Latino had hung up.

Luigi quickly dialed Valeria's number, but there was no answer. He tried her university line, letting it ring for a long time. When he realized that his call would remain unanswered, he called Stevens.

Chapter 17

Elena was sitting at a table in the living room that evening, reading and taking notes, when Luigi came in. She looked at him with pleading eyes but knew only too well that no one could force her father back to bed. She thought of asking him to leave his cigarettes on the table, but realized the childish nature of her request and kept quiet.

When she saw him heading for the door she yelled out to him, calling him reckless and irresponsible. Luigi thought his daughter took some pleasure in insulting him. He kissed her on the forehead, told her not to worry, and made for College Street.

A luminous rain was falling, but no one seemed eager to avoid it; many just walked along at their leisurely pace, and in the long queue in front of the cinema some broke out in dance, while others shrieked in pleasure; no one was seeking shelter. Luigi was thinking about Valeria, feeling strangely better; the unhoped-for freshness in the air gave him renewed energy. Feeling at a safe distance from home, he stopped under the flashing marquee and lit up a du Maurier, relishing its warm, comforting smoke. A gentle breeze lulled the rain into a slant, and a few drops came to rest on his forehead. Luigi picked up his pace, checked in his pocket to see if his pill case was there, and after the first tentative puffs he allowed himself a full-bodied one. He had never carried a gun, but tonight he could probably use one. Thoughts of Valeria spurred his hatred for the Latino. Luigi picked up his pace and headed for the Convento Rico just further along on College Street. The Convento Rico was a famous gay nightclub in the area that attracted many straight people who went there to dance to old disco music, patiently waiting for the midnight show featuring transvestites lip-synching famous Spanish songs. Patrons made their way slowly into the club, lined up like the limos ferrying their nocturnal fauna along College Street, waiting for the traffic lights to turn green.

    Luigi approached the entrance to the Convento Rico only to be unceremoniously shoved inside by a bald bouncer in a yellow jacket. He took a few steps down and found himself in an enormous cellar crowded with young people with shaved heads in every nook and cranny of the place. In the billiard room male and female couples in tank tops kissed to the beat of the music while balancing a beer and a billiard cue in either hand. The walls of the nightclub, like the bodies of the patrons, seemed to shake to the rhythm of the loud music. On the dance floor dozens of couples danced to the beat of an old Bee Gees tune that was familiar even to Luigi. Throngs of *grimpeiros* crowded the bar while someone managed to break loose from the heap balancing a glass in his hand. Behind the bar three or four baristas toiled at piecework rhythms. Surprisingly enough Luigi did not find the crowd and the noise irritating or tiring; not even the bodies and proud, carnivalesque silhouettes of the transvestites, wearing wigs that towered above their heads, floating on high heels like gigantic sacred icons among the faithful. Luigi thought he might have caught sight of the Latino, but he was mistaken. He glanced at his watch; it was only 10:45. An agile, sinuous man held on tightly to the buttocks of a younger man with a shaved head; unperturbed by the crowd, they coiled together, joining and parting with abandon to the rhythm of a blind and drunken tango.

    Luigi sat down at one of the tables where he was flooded at regular intervals by a beam of light from a moving Fresnel hanging from the ceiling. The beacon made its rounds, illuminating briefly a dark corner throbbing with the frantic energy of tangled bodies before moving on and letting them plunge into darkness again. He sat facing away from the dance floor, hoping to catch the attention of a server among the dark, chaotic throng. Now and then he turned around to look at dancing couples. When he had left home Luigi had felt at ease with himself, as though seized by an elusive serenity, but now a troubling, anxious curiosity had crept up on him. Only now did he understand the risk he was running, but the thought did not scare him; on the contrary, when he turned to look over at the dance floor he saw a woman sitting in front of him. He shifted his gaze towards the dance floor, but with the corner of his eye he followed the contour of a long, nylon-clad leg to a high-heeled shoe. He understood in a flash and looked up.

"Surprised?"

"Maybe." Luigi *was* caught by surprise, and the sight of Lucio in drag unleashed in him a turmoil of new sensations, both physical and sentimental. He summoned up all of his previous experiences, called up all the contorted and death-shrunken victims he had seen in his long career, remembered all of the horrible and dangerous situations in which he had been involved as a protagonist or a witness, saw the congealed blood on the wall or the sidewalk, all in the effort to mask his surprise.

"Where is Valeria?" Luigi asked.

There was no answer from Lucio Marros.

"Why did you want to see me?" Luigi asked.

Lucio Marros moved closer to him, resting his face on his elbows, which were wrapped in the sleeves of a white sequined dress. Luigi took a close look at him. He felt a mounting fear when he saw the Peruvian's eyes, made up to look like those of an animal, a seductive serpent or the Medusa.

Luigi sensed an empty resonance in his chest cavity, as if all the organs had been carried off by a flash wave, a hurricane; sensed that the only thing left in that emptiness was an old, puffing heart, now covered in mud, gasping out its last spurts of sludge before becoming still.

"Why did you try to kill us?" Luigi asked, attempting to gain full control of his emotions.

"You are afraid, ha?" Lucio replied, in Italian twisted by a strong Spanish accent.

"Maybe," Luigi said in a steady voice, taking comfort in the familiar calm he had experienced only a few minutes ago. "It's not an everyday spectacle, coming face-to-face with a bullfighter in drag. But you were not that great as a bullfighter, and as a woman you leave a lot to be desired."

"*Bravo, Signor* Sasta. You are not a great detective or a great journalist either," he said, stretching out on his chair.

"Why did you kill him?" Luigi asked, point-blank.

"Easy on the questions, *señor investigator*. I did not kill anyone."

"It was you, Lucio, you planted a *puntillo* in the nape of his neck!" Luigi pressed on.

"In any case, my name is not Lucio. I am Gina."

"But why did you kill him? Was it on orders from Santamaria?"

"Listen to all your questions! You have something I need. Don't screw with me, give me the photograph and Gina will disappear."

He started humming along with the tune that they were playing in the club.

"*I need love, I need love, I need love.* Don't you need love, *Señor* Sasta? Instead of mucking about as a detective. No, you are too old, no more love for you."

"Why did you want to kill us?" Luigi asked, just as the beam of light held them in its embrace, freeze-framing them into an image of mutual hatred; Lucio Marros was the sphinx, Luigi Sasta tried to solve the riddle in his icy stare.

"Well, I've had some success with Valeria. A pretty one, yes, *Señor* Sasta? Don't tell me you are in love with her? Of course. Otherwise, why would you give a shit about a traitor. You are in love ... the old geezer in love with a girl younger than his own daughter. Hand over the photograph, *Señor* Sasta, and you'll never see me again."

"You better hope nothing's happened to her."

"Don't worry about her. *I need love* ... don't you like this tune, *Señor* Sasta?"

Luigi gathered all his strength, stood up from the chair and tried to hit Lucio Marros, but managed only to grab his wig, which he held in his hand. The beam of light embraced them once again, highlighting Lucio Marros's eyes crinkling into a frozen look of surprise, then hatred. Some kind of netting covered up the Latino's bunched-up hair.

The light moved on, leaving them in the dark, but Luigi was able to see the small gun in the Latino's hand.

"That's no way to treat a woman, *Señor* Sasta. We are going for a little walk now," he hissed.

Someone stopped to check out the scene, and Luigi pleaded with his eyes for help, but his attempt was swallowed up by the chaos of bodies and sounds.

"What photo are you talking about?"

"Your girlfriend did not get a chance to ask me twice. I was very mean to her, very. Let's go."

"You killed her, you bastard!"

Fearless, Luigi got up and bolted again against the Peruvian, but could not reach him and fell face down next to the leg of the table. He had no strength, in spite of his rage, in spite of his need for vengeance, in spite of the fact that he had come so close to finally solving the riddle. Everything swirled around him, everything was about to be engulfed by mud; one last spurt of sludge and his old engine would come to a dead stop. A feeling of injustice came over him as he realized he was powerless to do anything but look up at those long legs wrapped in nylons, bending grotesquely, then kneeling, until the Latino's body fell down, his face next to him. Luigi watched the Latino's mouth open to whisper something, maybe that old tune *I need love* ...

Pandemonium broke out. Luigi saw people rushing around him and the Latino. A table was overturned; glasses were broken, sending shards in their direction. The song droned on, a voice begging for love. Valeria was dead; the Latino's mouth whispered his need for love, *I need love*. His face contorted into a sudden jerk, his serpent's eyes turned to face Luigi before their light went out and blood flowed from his mouth. Luigi sensed Sergeant Stevens's fat face next to them, asking something.

Valeria ... he wanted to call out her name but could not form the words. Hurry, run to her house! He wanted to cry out, but not even a murmur left his mouth. Luigi fixed his gaze on the sphinx-like face of Lucio Marros; on the running mascara, the lipstick-drenched mouth, and he closed his eyes, not in horror but because exhaustion had finally overcome him.

Police kill Michael Karrier's assassin in a shootout at a local nightclub
MICHAEL KARRIER'S ASSASSIN KILLED IN A SHOOTOUT
By Marco Arazzi

Just like in an old western movie, complete with a shootout in a public saloon with people running for their lives and tables flying about, the police got the bad guy. Lucio Marros, Michael Karrier's assassin, had lured Luigi Sasta, editor of Stampa Italica, *to a gay nightclub on College Street, with the pretext of giving him further clues on the murder at the Art Gallery. But in reality Lucio Marros, a Peruvian with no fixed address, had set up the editor of* Stampa Italica *in order to kill him, as he had done only hours*

Between Rothko and 3 Windows

before with Valeria Furlon, Michael Karrier's partner, whose body was found in the women's washroom at York University.

The police, who were protecting the journalist as a result of a previous attempt by Lucio Marros to kill him, were able to intervene before another heinous murder could take place. The killer, seeing he was surrounded, fired a few rounds of his pistol but was downed by officers of the homicide squad before the horrified eyes of the patrons.

The motives for Marros's cold-blooded execution of Karrier are still shrouded in mystery, but Sergeant Stevens of the homicide squad expressed his satisfaction in exposing the assassin and, above all, he added, for saving the life of the Stampa Italica *journalist, who had played a major role in the solution of the case.*

Luigi Sasta, journalist and editor at Stampa Italica, *has been working for years with the police as a consultant, helping in the solution of dozens of cases, thereby gaining a reputation, both within the community as well as beyond it, as an investigative reporter. He is currently in hospital, recovering from open-heart surgery, a bypass to correct coronary artery disease that had been previously scheduled, but was moved forward as a result of the tragic events of the last few days.*

Karrier's live-in partner, York University professor Valeria Furlon, was also killed in cold blood by Marros, who beat her to death two days ago in a washroom of the university, before finishing her off with a sharp dagger, most likely the same weapon he used to murder her partner.

Michael Karrier, whose real name was Michele Carrieri, was an Italian immigrant who had been living in Canada for the past ten years; he was killed a few days ago by Marros, in an exhibition room at the Art Gallery of Ontario, with a single blow of a dagger to the nape of his neck.

According to the detectives working on this case, some elements are still under investigation, and the file will not be archived until full light is shed on the murders of Karrier and Furlon.

Chapter 18

Elena rented a room in the hospital to celebrate the success of her father's bypass, and a veritable procession of people turned up. The invite had been limited to friends and professional acquaintances; consular authorities, members of Parliament, *Stampa Italica* staff and police representatives were welcome, but no one, absolutely no one, Elena had made abundantly clear in her phone messages, was to offer a cigarette to her father!

Luigi felt weak, a little out-of-sorts, and, between handshakes and quick chats, he cast sidelong glances at the yellowish afternoon beyond the window. He felt he was to blame for Valeria's death, and it weighed heavily on him, like the remorse that had eaten away at Michele Carrieri, killed in the Gallery just around the corner from the hospital.

As he was lost in his melancholy thoughts, his publisher reached out to him, placing his hand on his shoulder, telling him to get back to the paper. Luigi looked at him in silence, and only then did the publisher burst out into a laugh, saying he was joking, adding that Luigi could take as long a vacation as he needed before returning to the paper.

No one, the publisher said, no one, he emphasized, would ever sit at his desk. In the corner, staff from *Stampa Italica*, balancing plates with the mandatory slices of cake on them, were discussing the decisive victory of the second game by the Italian team. Arazzi was restless and looked about for an excuse to leave the room so he could go for a cigarette. Finally he left the soccer fans and walked down to the front garden, followed by Luigi's envious gaze, he would have loved to join him for a smoke. He was so helpless without the comfort of a du Maurier. The publisher took his leave, yelling out "Great job, Sasta!" but Luigi dampened his enthusiasm, whispering as firmly as he could that it wasn't over yet. The publisher turned back, saying nothing at first, then looked at Luigi with a great big question mark on his face and burst out into a loud laugh. In spite of Arazzi's article and the publisher's naive wishes, the Carrieri case would remain unsolved until Luigi signed off on it. Luigi reflected on these resolutions as he observed his daughter Elena unwrapping gifts, cutting cakes, and offering coffee and biscuits. It was clear as the light of day that Lucio Marros had killed Michele, but the reason and the motive were still a mystery. As far as Luigi was concerned, the case had been put on hold. He was certain that his pigheadedness would not be appreciated by the Consul, who was busy making a speech to all the guests praising Luigi's professional and human virtues – a journalist committed to the search for truth, but also to promoting the Italian language and the values of *italianità*: courage and hard work. Luigi, meanwhile, looked on from his armchair like a worker forced into early retirement, sent home with the gift of a gold-plated watch.

"Speech, speech," everyone cried out. Prompted by the acquiescent gaze of his staff, the plaintive sadness of *Signorina* Arianna's eyes, the Teflon faces of the authorities and the rusty smiles of the politicos, Luigi felt obliged to say a few words.

"If I am to be a new man," Luigi began slowly, "I might wish to surround myself with new people, but as nothing has changed other than a contraption in my chest, I am happy to be among so many friends. I've been wanting for a long time to take some time off, and it seems that the appropriate moment for a long vacation has come ... maybe even, who knows, in Italy. Maybe the time has come for me to return to that village in the Marches, whose whereabouts and name are unknown to you, but I can assure you that a sunset on those hills is worth more than ..." The word remained unspoken, but he saw it in his mind's eye, floating on a wave of blood, forcing him to stop and stare at Sergeant Stevens, who looked back at him inquisitively. "Maybe it's time to surrender to old age, to reclaim all the interests that our life's journey did not allow us to cultivate, and that is what I wish to do. Finally I can return to my passion for criminology, which I have always wanted to study in depth." Sergeant Stevens cracked a sardonic smile. "Or even anthropology, because I would like to write a book on our blessed community. In any case, I wish to thank you all for your show of affection and leave you with a promise." Luigi had wanted to break out into a river of words but held back.

... I promise that Carrieri's murder will not remain unsolved, that I will continue to seek the truth: that I owe this to Sergeant Stevens; to Giovanni and his coffee, which for thirty years I was not allowed to drink without drenching it in sugar; to Arazzi, who smokes in secret and who secretly wants my head; to our Consul who wants to stop receiving phone calls from the Ambassador and from Santamaria's friends; to my publisher, who, if he is to survive, will need funding from the Italian government but wants no more phone calls from the Consul, from the Ambassador and the politicos, who in turn do not cherish to be seen as criminals and who don't want to see their community criminalized; to Elena, who believes I am a has-been, but who spent many terrible nights offering me her heart to make up for mine; and above all to Valeria Furlon, who was able to feel unconditional love and who died for it ...

But he said none of this, leaving them instead with the promise that he would retire to a life of idleness worthy of Sallust.

As soon as he was done speaking everyone approached him; many offered an embrace, others a handshake or a kiss, and within minutes they all left the room, save for Elena, Giovanni, *Signorina* Arianna and Sergeant Stevens.

"Think about getting some rest; don't obsess any longer on the Karrier case. Good idea to study criminology," Sergeant Stevens said unconvincingly.

"I'll call you in a few days," Luigi replied, without waiting for an answer from his friend.

But the Sergeant spoke anyway. "I'm well aware of it," he said and went away with a smile.

Giovanni, his head hanging low, approached Luigi and said, "*Aim gona missiu!*"

"I know, thank you, Giovanni, but we'll see each other again," Luigi said, giving Giovanni a warm handshake and a pat on his back.

Signorina Arianna said only a few words. "I've brought you the mail."

"Thank you," Luigi Sasta replied, adding, "I have not forgotten that I promised you a gift. You are the only one working at *Stampa Italica* with an open heart and mind."

"Thank you, *Dottore*."

Luigi stepped over to the great window, while in the room Giovanni, *Signorina* Arianna and Elena started cleaning up in silence.

The ochre-tinged afternoon melted into dark brown, and the rain came. People leaving the hospital scampered towards the streetcar stop. The government building facing the window looked like a teapot about to boil over. Giovanni and *Signorina* Arianna left in silence. Elena approached her father and wrapped her arms around his waist.

"Don't be sad, *Papà*."

"I am not sad ... or maybe I am. Valeria Furlon was about your age, you know."

"It's not your fault, *Papà*."

"No. You're wrong. It's entirely my fault," Luigi said, tightening his hand around the parcel of letters. Like falling stars, raindrops glided down the glass of the large window. For the first time in many years Luigi felt a tear running down his cheek.

Chapter 19

Five young men, standing on a thin carpet of sand, leaned against the barrier of the bullring. Michele Carrieri smiled, as did Raul Santamaria, who hugged him, and a third young man who in turn was hugging a fourth. They were all about twenty-five years old, and all four of them had big smiles on their faces. Behind them a young *torero*, standing probably on a stool or a step, held the bull's ears up high, waving them in triumph. It was Lucio Marros, the man who had killed Michele and Valeria and who had tried to kill Luigi Sasta as well. Resting on his hospital bed, Luigi read once again the letter that came with the picture.

My Dear Signor *Sasta,*

Michael was the best man I ever met. In the past he had made mistakes, maybe even terrible ones, which I could only guess at by catching a sudden flash in his eyes, but the man I knew was no longer Michele Carrieri, he was Michael Karrier. The truth, as I mentioned to you that day, is that Michael was the love of my life.

I had time to get to know you and appreciate your strength and honesty, and for this reason I am sending you this picture. It may tell you more than it ever told me. I confess I lied to you; I did have the picture, and I knew that the truth is hiding in it. I don't know why I lied to you. I think I wanted justice to prevail as well as to seek vengeance for Michael's death, but it is also true that I wanted to protect him. I find it difficult to explain.

I beseech you to persevere in seeking the truth, the same truth, I am certain of it now, for which Michael wanted to return to Italy.

I understood all this thanks to you. I knew that one day Michael would have told me everything, and I kept waiting for it every time I saw in his eyes that flash tinged with remorse and a desire for justice to be done.

I had known for a while that Michael Karrier had been Michele Carrieri, but I never questioned him, not even when my curiosity was eating me alive. Can you understand this, Signor Sasta?

A warm embrace,
Valeria Furlon

P.S. I have entrusted this letter to a student, asking him to mail it, in case something happened to me.

Luigi thought back to the student and smiled. He looked at the letter and read the signature one more time. He felt old and dirty, even with his new, patched-up heart, old and dirty.

He turned to face the window, which opened onto a dark brick wall, and wept. This time the tears flowed freely, and he broke into redeeming sobs that came from faraway, from Mariuccia's death and the failure of his career, to his backing down to the City's powers that be and the flight for his life at the Harris Water Filtration Plant. In the end, though he felt better, an explosive, pent-up anger overcame him.

He called Sergeant Stevens but, as he was not in his office, left a voicemail message asking him to join him as soon as possible in the hospital. He read the letter one more time, then let it slip to the floor and returned to studying the picture. On the back he read: "Lima, *Feria del Señor de los Milagros*, October 19, 1975. Michele, Raul, Tino, Beppe, Lucio."

The picture seemed to have been taken in the bullring. He knew the solution to Michele Carrieri's murder was in the picture. A cigarette might help him out. The phone rang. Luigi picked up.

"Hello?"

"What is it now, Sasta? Shouldn't you be resting?" Sergeant Stevens asked.

"There's plenty of time to rest. Get over here quickly. I think I have discovered Karrier's assassin."

"We already know him; it's the Peruvian!"

"Yes, but we have no motive, and I believe I have found it."

"OK. I'll come tonight, only make sure your daughter won't be there, or she'll kill me!"

"Not to worry, she's at her house."

"I am coming, you old maniac!"

The Sergeant hung up. Luigi listened for a while to the groans in the corridor, then fell asleep.

Investigation into Michael Karrier's murder follows Italian lead
ITALIAN POLITICS BEHIND MURDER AT THE ART GALLERY
By Luigi Sasta

The Karrier murder case is far from over. In spite of the haste shown by some of the investigators, the media and the political authorities, the death of Lucio Marros, Michael Karrier's assassin, forestalls any attempts to resolve issues arising out of the gruesome murder that took place at the Art Gallery of Ontario, and the even more horrific killing of Michael Karrier's partner, who was beaten to death while at work.

The death of Lucio Marros at the hands of the police, who were able to stop him from committing a third murder, prevents us from obtaining answers to some questions but allows us to speculate on some issues.

Valeria Furlon, a professor in the Foreign Languages faculty at York University, was not only very beautiful, elegant and cultured; she was an enchanting woman, full of life and love, and it is for love that she lost her life.

Those who met Valeria Furlon after the death of her partner were reminded of a tragic figure from the classical Greek theatre, a fragile creature whose life could be broken at any given moment and in defence of which she could only offer her love.

The detectives are still in the dark about Michael Karrier's past, and it is possible that Valeria Furlon herself did not know very much either, but after the death of her partner she had told someone, the only person she trusted, that she would have protected Michael with her own life. And this is what she did.

Following the murder of Michael Karrier, the police searched the house he shared with Valeria Furlon and noted that a picture had been removed from a wall. Valeria had said that it was a print of a painting by Mark Rothko, a painter from the fifties; this painting had been framed in a shop whose name she had forgotten.

This turned out to be false: it was a photograph of the young Michele Carrieri and some of his friends in Peru, among whom was his murderer, Lucio Marros.

Why had Valeria misled the investigative team? Probably because the photograph held the key with which to unlock Michele Carrieri's past, the man also known as Michael Karrier, with whom she shared her life.

The lie, and especially the missing photograph, cost Valeria her life at the hands of Marros, who tortured her to death in the hope of obtaining the incriminating photograph. Why else, we ask, would anyone kill for a photograph of a young group of friends?

But Valeria Furlon could not hand over the photograph because she had mailed it to someone who may be unable to ever forgive himself for failing to grasp what was about to happen and step in to prevent it.

Who was pictured in the photograph?

In addition to the Peruvian murderer, there was a famous Italian politician whose image also appeared in an article

Corrado Paina

discovered in Michael Karrier's wallet the day he was killed. All of the clues lead to Italy, to people and events that probably took place there.

Chapter 20
June 26

In spite of everyone's advice to the contrary, the doctor, Elena, Sergeant Stevens, who pretended to worry but in reality was rooting for him, and the publisher, who was wary of potential problems with Italian authorities, Luigi departed from Toronto and landed at Milano Lunate Airport the following afternoon, where, under a blazing sun, he joined a rippling, nervous queue and waited for a taxi. The next day Italy was scheduled to play the quarterfinals. Luigi looked on at the crowd in the queue: elegant and beautiful people, different from what he observed in Canada, where people frequently took up their place in the queue in grim and dark silence. This was a colourful, clamouring crowd with cellphones ringing out like whistles in a demonstration: some called their families to tell them they were on their way home, many complained about the heat, others about the labour strikes, and the rest, the majority, were busy discussing the games. Luigi lowered his eyes to cast a glance at the sum total of his summer wardrobe: the single-button, threadbare, grey summer wool suit he was wearing, plus an old brown linen shirt. For the first time in his life he was ashamed of his appearance. He felt out of place among these fashionably dressed, fragrant people waiting for a taxi. Finally it was his turn. A young balding man with the look of a bank manager, wearing a garish, colourful short-sleeved shirt over pallid forearms, stopped his car, bolted out like a cat, grabbed his luggage and stored it in the trunk.

"Where are we off to, *Signor?*" He smiled at Luigi, who was busy inspecting the cleanliness inside the vehicle. What a difference from the Toronto taxis, with their sagging fenders, their threadbare seats and drivers whose knowledge of the streets left a lot to be desired. Luigi asked the driver to bring him to Hotel Splendour, then sank in his seat and basked in the perfectly controlled temperature of the air-conditioned car.

"That's at the Central Railway Station, right?" asked the driver, who was weaving in and out of traffic heading for downtown Milan. "Do you have a favourite route?"

"Your choice," Luigi replied and returned to looking beyond the car window at the city going by.

"Do you mind if I smoke?" the driver asked.

"Not at all," Luigi said. "Light one up for me also."

"I am in the habit of asking my passengers if it's OK to smoke. I don't like the stench of smoke in the car. You never know, it might irritate some people ..."

"But it's not a stench, more like an aroma, like a good coffee."

"If you say so," the driver said and lit up an MS.

Luigi took in a full breath, filling his lungs with smoke while the driver reached for the ringing cellphone.

"Hello ... yes ... yes, it can be done. I'll drop off a passenger at the station and ... yes, the Central. OK, I'll be there in ten minutes." The driver flipped his phone shut. "My apologies about the cellphone."

"Not to worry, I don't mind cellphones, but unfortunately here in Italy I cannot use my own, it does not work. Having a cellphone once saved my life, you know."

"That's a good one, you should tell me all about it," the driver said.

"No, better not." On the Via Romagna, Luigi looked up at the austere palaces and the trees shrouded in thick smog.

"I'm sorry, but am I right in thinking that you don't live in Italy but you are Italian?" Without missing a beat the taxi driver yelled out "Prick!" to the driver of a car speeding by at 80 km an hour. "Please excuse my vulgarity," he said, "but some people should not be allowed to drive."

"I agree with you," Luigi said.

"So, your cellphone does not work here in Italy ..."

"I am from Canada," Luigi replied, laconically, fascinated by the skill of the driver who miraculously, managed to avoid collisions by anticipating, with the appropriate profanity, the reactions of other drivers, while navigating through the traffic like a torpedo in a Milan that looked to Luigi like a bottomless, crowded ocean. Still focused on the long line of cars heading towards the traffic lights on the way to a huge piazza surrounded by tall buildings sporting gigantic advertisements, he added, "To make a long story short, so as not to bore you, I'll tell you that I was able to call the police just in time before someone managed to kill me; were it not for a cellphone, I would not be here to tell you about it."

"Canada is beautiful. I'd really like to go there," the driver said. Luigi's story did not seem to be of any interest to him.

"I am surprised; do you know much about Canada?"

"I've read some things because I like to travel. I've been to Asia, to Africa, the USA and even to South America, but never to Canada. I'm not really a taxi driver, though the work is good, and it leaves me free to do other things. I have a degree in philosophy and am waiting for something more appropriate, otherwise you can go crazy working like this, in this hard and difficult city, even for people like me ... born and bred, I mean. Do you know where we are now?"

"No."

"We are in Piazza Loreto," the driver said.

"They killed Mussolini here," Luigi said quietly.

"No. This is where they strung him up and his lover Petacci. As I was saying, this is very stressful work, particularly in this city. This used to be a great city, but today it is disgusting, a brothel ..."

155

"Why so?"

"You'll see for yourself as soon as you go for a walk. Take a look in front of the railway station; Africans, Albanians, rejects from all over the world. It's enough to ..."

"In Toronto we also have people from everywhere, all races and languages."

"And how do they all get along, these people?"

Luigi could not come up with a quick reply, asking himself, how do they get along? All we can say, he thought, is that they spend the day together at work, before going their own way, that in the end they did not really know one another. "I would say that they make the best of it, they try to get along as best they can," Luigi finally volunteered.

"Not here, it's not at all like that here," the driver jumped in. "Not at all, here, no way! They're all good-for-nothings. See, look to that traffic light up ahead, see the flower vendors, the beggars, the squeegee kids. It's all the government's fault. They should have sent them all back as soon as they crossed the border – I don't mean to say they are all lazy or criminals, but the great majority are drug dealers and pimps, and Italy is sinking into –"

"I'm sorry to interrupt," Luigi said. "Do you know the address of the Independent Party headquarters?"

"Of course I know it, dear sir, I am a member of the Independent Party. But why do you want to know it, if I may ask?"

"I am to meet one of your party's members of Parliament," Luigi replied, without a hint of enthusiasm.

"You are not looking for ..." the driver asked, turning his head to scrutinize the passenger.

"I am going to meet the Honourable Raul Santamaria. Do you know him?"

"Do I know him? Of course I know him, he is our leader, a self-made man who was born into poverty in one of the toughest working-class neighbourhoods, growing up among people who worked all their lives, among the *terroni*, but he rolled up his sleeves to his elbows and look where he is now ..."

"Yes, of course," Luigi replied. "Is this the railway station?" he asked, pointing to a huge white marble building with an Eiffel-type green metal roof that reminded him of the Harris Water Filtration Plant and, consequently, of Valeria.

"Yes, sir. So you are going to see Santamaria," the driver said, wiping away Luigi's meandering thoughts. "Good for you! Tell him Gino the taxi driver sends his regards."

"I'll be sure to do that. Can I ask you a question? Why don't you ask him for a job, seeing as you know him?" Luigi said, getting out of the car in front of the Hotel Splendour.

Gino bolted out in his usual manner and stopped Luigi from reaching into the trunk. "Let me take care of that, a man of your age, no offence ..."

"Thank you," Luigi said in a fog, taking out his wallet.

"Thank you, *Signore*, there is no need. We are not in Rome here. Please give my regards to the Honourable Santamaria."

Gino, who had dashed out to his car after giving the luggage to a hotel porter, looked up from his seat at Luigi, handing him a business card. "Should you need anything, please call me at this number," he said and plunged into the roaring traffic heading towards the Central Railway Station.

Luigi proffered his documents to the hotel clerk and was taken up to his room. He removed his jacket and shirt, and opened the window. The heat did not bother him, and even though he felt tired, he was able to focus on his thoughts, which became gentler as he basked in the sun's reflection off the white marble of the station. Leaning out on the small balcony, Luigi took out the taxi driver's business card and read:

Gino Barbieri
Taxi Driver
Tel ...

He looked out to the poplars fluttering in the breeze and sensed the damp fragrance of leaves rising up towards him from some cellar. Since he had stopped smoking his other senses had become sharper, especially his senses of smell and taste, which triggered in him the familiar primordial hunger that as the child of immigrants he knew so well. Now, he was overcome by that unmistakable mingling of human and natural fragrances. From the window he could see two kiosks, one of which was submerged in a fluttering sea of blue and tri-colour flags.

Luigi moved away from the window and made for the bathroom. He took off his undershirt and looked at the reflection of his scar in the mirror. His stitches, which were to be removed shortly, seemed alive to Luigi (perhaps because of the pale burgundy light in the room), like ants crawling on the left side of the sternum, thanks to the fact that the open-heart bypass surgery had been performed without the full opening of the chest cavity. They had fixed his old heart. He would do the same with the old Subaru once back in Toronto.

In spite of his tiredness, his thoughts were lucid, but above all his suffering seemed to have come to a full stop. He was close, he sensed, very close to the truth, to the motive behind Carrieri's murder, to that Santamaria that the taxi driver idolized as a man with "cojones." "We're almost there," Luigi said, looking at himself in the mirror. He leaned over the sink, splashed water on his underarms, washed his face, downed a couple of blood-thinners, grabbed a fresh undershirt and pyjamas from the suitcase, changed into them, closed the window, pulled the curtains, turned on the air conditioning and went to bed. He soon fell asleep, lulled by the nervous sound of car horns going by.

Chapter 21

Luigi woke up feeling rejuvenated. He left his room around five, took the elevator, caught a glimpse of his old suit in the mirror and was overcome by the familiar sense of shame, which he attenuated by promising himself to buy a new one. On the ground floor he approached the reception counter, bathed in the soft light coming from a night lamp, and watched as a sleepy hotel clerk struggled with a runaway printer spitting out bills non-stop. It was still dark when he left the hotel, and the air was fresh. Dark and gangly lampposts illuminated his way. He was riding waves of energy and lusted for a coffee and croissant.

Luigi inhaled the unexpected fragrance of the leaves, breathing in the breeze that fluttered the branches and blew a newspaper along the sidewalk. He wended his way towards the railway station. He walked through an archway where, parked in the orange glow of overhead lamps, taxi drivers were asleep. Luigi did not stop to ask for directions and headed towards the Central Station's interior. He came to a bar where patrons silently stirred their spoons in their espressos or cappuccinos. Streetcar conductors, taxi drivers, passengers, homeless old men, an innocent beardless face or two belonging to sleep-deprived teenagers ... A barista with the face of a ferret made an espresso for him and offered him the sugar bowl, which Luigi pushed away, thinking back to Giovanni, who always insisted on drowning his coffee in sugar.

The server asked him to choose his own croissant from the display window on the counter where they were neatly arranged according to their filling: pastry cream, chocolate or marmalade. He was tempted by all of them but finally opted for the croissant with pastry cream filling which, in his view, no one in Toronto knew how to prepare. They were splendid, delicious, delicate croissants, unlike their gigantic and arrogant Canadian counterparts, butter-splattered concoctions conceived and executed to appeal to raw hunger, to the point of suffocating nausea.

The barista went back to his discussion of the national team's game with another patron, and Luigi turned to look beyond the bar window at Piazza Amedeo d'Aosta, where a bus was unloading workers on their way to their jobs, more than likely in faraway places, Luigi thought, given the time. A group of Africans milled about in front of a watermelon stand. The women, he was sure, were prostitutes. A few men, scrawny, blond and dirty, Albanians or Yugoslavs for sure, were fast asleep on the flowerbeds in the piazza. One of them got up from his grassy pallet and marched to the water fountain to wash his underarms. He yawned and stretched out his arms, straightening his back. Other young men, their faces emaciated, scampered aimlessly about the piazza like rats in search of food. The aroma coming from the espresso machine puffing out steam, and the busy chatter of patrons echoing in the large bar, fuelled his rising good humour. His breakfast over, Luigi paused to look longingly at the remaining croissants in the display case and promised to himself that he would try a new flavour each morning. He smiled at his old man's gluttony and made for the main piazza in front of the station where, on its white marble pavement, he thought he recognized the nocturnal dwellers of the station, unmistakable because of their droopy eyes and slow, aimless walk; a far cry from the hurried pace of those going to their jobs.

Luigi rambled about for a while before stopping at a kiosk that sold all manner of pornographic magazines. He bought a newspaper, and when he picked it up he noticed it had been piled on top of one such magazine, which he glanced at with a sincere shyness.

"Do you sell more papers in this way?" Luigi asked the newsvendor, an older man with the face of an aging Pekingese.

There was no reply from the newsvendor, who probably had not understood the question and stared at Luigi just long enough to accept payment.

Luigi made his way towards the subway station under a dark mantle of night that was shredding into gashes of red light through which oozed a bluish liquid. The subway was still closed. Luigi asked a pedestrian for directions to Corso Buenos Aires, who in turn asked Luigi for a coin or two; he did not refuse, more out of shock, he thought, than for any humanitarian instinct.

On his way Luigi came across a prostitute getting into a taxi, on her way home after a night's work; a couple of distinguished gentlemen with their dogs; and an older woman feeding pigeons who flocked up and down in the air like an umbrella opening and closing. The metal shutters of the bars lining the street rolled up noisily, and the stands in the local market were opening up for business, while some men unloaded vans full of hundreds of t-shirts and flags sporting the colours of the Italian national team. The city was getting ready for a big celebration. A group of black men in a corner was busy sharing a watermelon.

He glanced at his watch and decided to take the subway downtown. As if by tacit agreement among the citizens of Milan, like a sudden changing of the guards, the underground corridors of the subway were flooded with people, and the entry doors snapped open with loud noises, sending a symphony of mechanical sounds upwards into the vaults. A stench of urine assaulted Luigi's nostrils. He bought a booklet of tickets, went through the doors and sat down on the bench in a crowd of silent people busily reading the paper or struggling to keep awake while waiting for the train to arrive.

On his many previous trips to the city Luigi recalled seeing dozens of working-class commuters carrying lunch boxes, but the times had changed, and none of the passengers were working class; they were all early-rising professionals. Luigi took his seat and proceeded to cast a sidelong glance at the newspaper belonging to another passenger, only to have his reading interrupted by a plaintive voice. A girl was crying out that she was hungry and needed money. She walked through the silent, indifferent crowd holding out her hand; only Luigi and another passenger gave her some coins.

Is this what happens in large metropolises, or is it just this city? Luigi asked himself. In Toronto he had never witnessed anything like it. To be sure, the streets saw their share of beggars and homeless people sleeping on the grates by the subway stations, but he had never seen such a blatantly theatrical begging for money met with such total indifference from the crowd, as though it were a normal, everyday scene. His musings came to a sudden stop as people elbowed their way to the Duomo Station stop, pushing Luigi along until the train vomited him out onto the platform. He managed to reach the exit, and, just as he cleared the last step leading to the open air, he looked up in amazement at Duomo. A few pedestrians ambled about, dwarfed by the immense monument, unexpectedly grey-white, like the Central Railway Station. That was not the only thing these two monuments had in common, even though the Duomo stood like a fountain in deep freeze, while the station reminded him of a frozen mammoth from Neolithic times. Both provided a gathering place for migrants, refugees, faceless people in perpetual motion, people Luigi knew about but who stood out violently here in Milan, like a splash of colour on a reluctant neutral background, as though the subject, the background, the canvas and the frame refused in vain to accept their presence. A small crowd of Africans had set up shop in front of the Duomo peddling cigarette lighters, videotapes and flags, hats and t-shirts featuring the national soccer team. Luigi ambled about for an hour or two before deciding to call Raul Santamaria from a public telephone.

"Independent Party, good morning."

"Good morning. Could I speak to the Honourable Santamaria –"

"Who's calling?"

"Luigi Sasta, editor-in-chief of *Stampa Italica* from Toronto."

"Thank you."

After a few bars of background music, Luigi recognized Santamaria's voice. "Good morning. You don't give up easily, I see."

Luigi offered no reply.

"What do you want from me?" Santamaria asked.

"I'm in Milan and I would like to meet with you ... for an interview." Santamaria did not seem surprised at all.

"Since I don't seem to be able to discourage you, why don't you drop by the party headquarters this afternoon and we'll do the interview. Then we can watch the game."

"To tell the truth, I am not a fan of soccer. Why don't we meet tomorrow?"

"OK. Tomorrow morning in my office we'll be able to talk calmly."

"Thank you, Honourable Member."

"Don't mention it! You've noticed our bright, sunny weather here in Milan ..."

"The sun shines brightly in Canada as well."

"Of course. I'll leave you now, if that's all right, and I'll see you tomorrow!"

Luigi was, once again, left holding the receiver in his hand. He dialed another number, and, after many rings, a sleepy, rude voice picked up. Luigi spoke only for a few seconds before hanging up. He went for a short walk, stopping in Via Torino, where he bought a double-breasted blue suit, and a shirt and tie. That afternoon, Luigi thought, he might buy a pair of shoes. He left the store, stopped in a bank to exchange some money and finally hailed a taxi. "The Splendour Hotel!" he called out to the driver, who lost no time in snaking his way into the traffic.

It was sweltering. Luigi opened the window. Two boys on a motor scooter, one of whom was busily waving an Italian flag, rode by him, blocking his view of the colonnade of the church of San Lorenzo. Luigi rolled the window closed to shut out the acrid smell of dust and smoke that parched his throat. He floated on a wave of enthusiasm; he would rest for a while, and later he would meet with Tino Magnasco at a pizzeria on one of the canals.

Chapter 22

"Then one fine day Comasina was awash in the stuff, probably because the Mafia bosses had been sent into house arrest, and you could find it everywhere in the neighbourhood, in the large and small factories, and all along the busy highway. Or simply because the stuff had appeared all over Milan," Tino Magnasco said to Luigi as he poured himself another glass of white. It was a sweltering, noisy day. They sat at a table in a crowded pizzeria on one of the canals just a few steps from the dock, which was swarmed by people who had gathered at a spot overlooking the confluence of waters from the canals. The summer excitement had been given a boost by another resounding victory by the Italian national team, securing its place in the quarterfinals.

"So you all knew each other, you were friends?" Luigi showed Tino the photograph.

"We were more than friends, especially Raul and Michele. They were very close, but all four of us were very good friends."

"Who is the *torero*?" Luigi pointed to Marros waving the bull's ears in the air.

"Exactly ... he was a *torero*," Tino Magnasco said in a whisper.

"Was he your friend?"

"We met him that day. We saw each other a few times while we were in Lima, then I lost track of him, but I think Raul and Michele kept in touch."

"How do you know that?"

"The only thing I know is that, once our group broke up, the two of them continued to make trips to Peru." Tino

Magnasco turned his stupefied gaze on the envelope that Luigi had handed to him and paused, before checking the contents.

"You don't see Santamaria anymore?" Luigi asked, brusquely, somewhat irritated by Tino's obscene gesture.

"How much is in here?" Tino Magnasco asked.

"Three million, but there could be more ... and Santamaria?"

"Ah, yes ... back to Santamaria. How much more?"

"What do you mean?"

"How much more money is there?"

"Let's say double," Luigi replied.

"In exchange for what?"

"Listen, let's get things straight, I am looking only for specific information. I am a journalist."

"Bullshit. Who are you?" Tino Magnasco raised his voice.

"I am a journalist." Luigi repeated in a monotone.

Tino Magnasco struggled to get up, saying, "Look, you can keep your money," and threw the envelope on the table.

"Wait – let me finish." Luigi reached out to grab his arm.

"Go on, talk ... but make sure you say something useful, otherwise it's goodbye, nice to meet you," threatened Tino Magnasco, pushing Luigi's hand away.

"Michele Carrieri is dead!" Luigi said, looking straight into the alcoholic haze of Tino Magnasco's eyes. "Michele was killed, and I am here to find out why."

In spite of the crowd in the pizzeria with groups of children waving their flags as they swarmed among the patrons, Luigi felt a sudden silence envelope them, protecting them from the noisy racket.

"When?" Tino Magnasco let himself fall into his chair.

"Three weeks ago," Luigi said in a low voice.

"Where?" Tino Magnasco lowered his gaze to look at the glass in front of him.

"In Toronto, in Canada."

"What was Michele doing there?"

"He lived with a woman, had changed his name. He was doing well, but ..."

Tino Magnasco raised his eyes to look at Luigi. "But?!"

"He wanted to return to Italy, he wanted to confess, to tell the truth ... which you know ..."

"I don't know what you're talking about. Who killed him?"

"The Peruvian," Luigi whispered.

"Lucio ..."

"Yes, Lucio Marros," Luigi interrupted Tino Magnasco. "I believe he had received some money from Raul and Michele. The same Lucio who was involved with guerrilla groups, as most of the boys in the group were in those times. It's possible that Michele wanted to return to Italy to tell the truth about the source of that money ..."

"What are you implying? There is no proof. The bastards! They killed Michele. I had not seen him for such a long time. He was a friend ..."

Luigi was losing his patience. "Who killed him?"

"You've already said it yourself, the goddamned Peruvian!"

"I'm asking: who gave the order to kill him?" Luigi signalled for another bottle of wine. "Maybe those who might end up in jail if Michele had confessed?"

"All of us would have had to pay for it, my dear sir!" Tino Magnasco lowered his head onto his crossed arms on the table and shifted his gaze to the envelope, which he started to fondle.

Luigi poured him another glass. "Tell me about it, *Signor* Magnasco ..."

"Not here." Tino downed his wine in one gulp and got up from the table.

"Let's go for a walk," he said.

On leaving the pizzeria they were swarmed by a mob of flag-wavers singing out loud to the moon. Across the water a large crane shimmered in the moonlight. They hailed a taxi, and Tino Magnasco asked the driver to take them to the Comasina. Luigi was calm, in spite of feeling tired. He felt he was getting closer to the truth. The real truth: not the truth of Ibsen's "vital lie," which he quoted from memory even though he had never really read Ibsen, and which he used in his quarrels with Mariuccia and lately with his daughter Elena.

Tino Magnasco had the appearance of a man in a state of hypnosis, his absent gaze lost somewhere beyond the window, which Luigi understood and respected; the appropriate response of grief at the loss of Michele. Luigi's gaze absorbed the landscape flowing by his window: the ever-changing urban cityscape. They drove past the ancient palaces, past the illuminated shop windows towards one of the darker, characterless suburbs, like the ones in Toronto; greasy, smoky areas that could unsettle anyone but Luigi, especially now. Prostitutes were stationed all along these arterial roads in which cars scurried about like relentless cockroaches preparing their attack. The moment he'd been waiting for had arrived: he was about to come face-to-face with the final truth. Luigi wondered if he really wanted to know.

Tino Magnasco broke the silence to give some final directions to the taxi driver, who drove them to a hillside meadow close to a highway bridge just behind tall and anonymous condominium buildings. Tino Magnasco handed a one-hundred-thousand lire banknote to the driver and asked him to wait for their return. Luigi followed him. They climbed the hillside, passing by small wooden huts standing guard over shabby little vegetable gardens. Tino stopped when they reached the crest of a small rise. Luigi was right behind him.

"This is where Beppe died," Tino Magnasco said in a cold, indifferent tone, kicking a pebble that went rolling down the escarpment.

Luigi fixed his gaze on the rolling pebble.

"It was a different night, rainy, although here at the Comasina, I don't know why, but I don't remember ever seeing the sun." Tino Magnasco pulled out a hipflask from his pocket and took a gulp.

"He died here; we took him here, Raul, Michele, and I, and we killed him."

Tino threw away his hipflask and made for the taxi.

Luigi's eyes followed the hipflask's trajectory in the escarpment. The truth he had so badly sought, the truth that would redeem Michele Carrieri, was much more horrible than he had imagined. Luigi could see Michele Carrieri's remorse, the escarpment that never left his mind, not even in Valeria's embrace, nor when he walked home from his job. Not even on Sunday outings to the country or dinners out. Luigi had not asked Tino Magnasco to wait for him. He heard the taxi leave, turned to see the car make for the bridge, then turned back to look at the hipflask: he felt an overwhelming sadness come over him, thinking that his own life, Beppe's life and Michele's shared a common thread.

He saw Valeria helping him along on the hill as they tried to outrun the Peruvian: Valeria, shimmering in the moonlight like the hipflask thrown away in that hole, rolling down the escarpment before being snuffed out by the darkness of the undergrowth. Poor Valeria, the sparks of her life snuffed out, lying in darkness like the hipflask, unable to bask in the light of the moon hiding behind the shoulders of the faceless condominium.

Chapter 23
June 28

Luigi felt good, even his relationship with the heat of the last few days before his operation had changed; it was no longer a monster that breathed down his neck relentlessly as he tried to move his tired, old body. The heat had returned, at times muggy, but a harbinger of summer happiness nonetheless. With his jacket draped over his arm, Luigi ambled quietly in the halls of the Ambrosiana, pausing in front of some paintings of the Lombard school, especially the Madonna and child of Melone. Baby Jesus amusing himself with his foot reminded him of Elena, who had spent endless hours on her bed examining her toes, playing the same game of cleaning her toes by sticking her index finger meticulously between them. Luigi and Mariuccia, relaxing on either side of the baby, basked in the diligent and determined performance of her task. Luigi had not been lured to the Ambrosiana by Melone's canvas; his real interest lay in a small still-life painting. Finally he could enjoy it in total calm. Unlike in other still-life canvases (Luigi hated the German and Flemish schools, with their penchant for dead and bloodied pheasants and hares), in this one the subject was not frozen but imbued with life until the moment of death, noticeable in the fleeting sense of decay and the decadence of muted hues. He stopped in front of it for several minutes, in spite of the cacophonous arrival of a school group singing out a popular movie theme and the churlish hordes of tourists and visitors who had little taste for Caravaggio's still life. Luigi had no reason to affect any expertise. He limited his observation of the painting to finding resonances with his own life experience. The inevitable process of decomposition of the barely visible fruit reminded him of Michele Carrieri's conversion, but in reverse. He was fully aware of the religious connotations of the word "conversion": was it possible that Michele's remorse had deep roots in religious stigma? Luigi Sasta would never be able to know.

That same morning Luigi had walked into the efficient and glossy headquarters of the Party of Independence and been welcomed by Raul Santamaria, in a far less aggressive manner than he recalled from their telephone encounter; much more reflective, with a deeper sense of doom.

A nervous, silent secretary showed Luigi into Santamaria's office.

"Sit down, sit down," Santamaria urged, without bothering to look in his direction. Luigi sat in front of a glossy desk showcasing many plaques and prizes that had been conferred on the Honourable Santamaria, the young lawyer and fearless canoeist. Santamaria was busy looking out the window beyond the clay-tiled roofs to the Duomo and the skyscrapers that were sprouting like wild mushrooms.

"I've always loved this city," Santamaria finally said, as though he were waking up from some deep, dark thought. "If I'm not mistaken, Milan is not very well-known in Canada, is it?" Santamaria continued on without waiting for a reply from Luigi, who in any case would not have offered one. "Canadians and Americans are better acquainted with Florence, Venice, Rome. They are unaware that the fate of the country is decided here, that Italians owe their sustenance to this place, that it is here that we pay taxes ..."

"And that's not all, Honourable Santamaria, much more goes on here," Luigi said in a low voice, thinking that Santamaria might turn to face him in anger. But this was not to be: the Honourable Santamaria, about forty-five years old with salt and pepper hair and a svelte and nervous body sporting a double-breasted suit, kept on talking, still looking out the window.

"We accomplish many things in life, we make many mistakes, and I can understand this, but I don't understand those who show repentance. You see, not repenting allows us to open up a parenthesis in which we say that there was a time in our life when we were not yet grown up, fully conscious and mature ... but no, we are obliged to be accountable, to be ruthless with ourselves and others ... But maybe you are not following me," he said, turning to look at Luigi, who smiled bitterly on seeing Santamaria's nervous demeanour.

"You are here to research the murder of Michele Carrieri, to write an article about it, so you too, like hordes of other journalists, can contribute to the current chaos in Italy. You wish to write about my past? Or are you here because of your sense of justice? If you are moved by a sense of justice then you should know that –"

"I am sorry to interrupt you, Honourable Santamaria," Luigi said. "You, Tino Magnasco and Michele Carrieri killed a man. It's not clear to me why, in this place, so maybe you can help me understand. I was not even acquainted with Michele Carrieri. I was called by a policeman friend of mine to help him out in this case – the police were in the habit of calling me every time an Italian was involved ... as victim or assassin, no matter. To tell you the truth, at first I thought of something completely different, the usual honour killing or Mafia settling of scores, but I was wrong. There was something different about this killing, starting with the victim, not your typical one, and then the scene of the crime. Think about it, in an art gallery. Lucio Marros might have chosen a different place, less dramatic, less in the public eye. I couldn't tell, but he may have had no choice due to Carrieri's very quiet life. And the singular, strange choice of weapon, a *puntillo* ... a little too symbolic for an ordinary crime of passion or a murder with an ordinary motive. Were it not for my friend's phone call, as

I mentioned, I would have no reason to be interested in this case. And there are other motives which I will tell you about later, if you like. Now, why don't you tell me the whole truth?" Luigi removed from an envelope the photograph that Valeria had sent him and placed it on the desk. "Do you remember this, Honourable Santamaria?"

"Yes, I remember it. I made a gift of it myself to Michele seven, eight years ago in Toronto …"

"And is this the reason for which you had Michele Carrieri killed?!" Luigi exclaimed. Santamaria was silent and kept looking at the photograph.

"We were all friends. It seems impossible that so much time has gone by … too much friendship … perhaps a friendship so deep could have no other outcome …"

"Honourable Santamaria, your friendship led to the death of Beppe Lucchi, a poor drug addict, and then to the murder of Michele Carrieri, and the execution of an innocent: Valeria Furlon, Michele Carrieri's life partner."

Santamaria glanced at the desk, then looked at Luigi with a bitter smile on his face.

"We all came from that accursed Comasina; drugs, crime and anger, a great deal of anger, a burning desire to escape without knowing how …"

Luigi was about to jump in but decided to let him go on. He took out a small recording machine from his pocket and placed it on the desk. Santamaria looked at the elegant little contraption and took it in his hand.

"You don't think I am going to speak into this, do you?"

"Is there a difference?" Luigi asked him.

"Maybe not, but you can always write what I am about to tell you."

"Honourable Santamaria, I could have written anything I wanted yesterday because you are a murderer. You ordered the murder of Michele Carrieri because he was planning to return to Italy to confess to the killing of Beppe Lucchi. He wanted to come back to Italy to see justice done, not out of remorse but because he could not stomach your hypocrisy, your politician's rhetoric, never mind the accountability you mentioned before. That is why he kept the article with your picture in it, the one in which you talk about your party and level accusations against Rome. Do you know when it finally clicked for me? Right after you told me on the phone that you had been to Toronto ..."

Santamaria attempted to cut in, but Luigi was determined to continue.

"So you met with him in Milan and understood that Michele Carrieri was serious in his intentions, because Valeria had changed him, love had triggered a strange mechanism ... But this was only a detail to you, so you asked Lucio Marros to help out, and he butchered him like he would a bull. You are a murderer. Whether you speak into the tape recorder or not is irrelevant, as you will have to talk to the police."

"You cannot understand," Santamaria whispered, looking at Luigi.

"Honourable Santamaria, you are a murderer."

***

Luigi looked again at the still-life painting. A leaf seemed on the verge of jumping out from the canvas, freeing itself from the background colour.

A little girl pulled on his pants and Luigi turned to look at her. "Sir, you dropped that envelope," the little girl said.

"Oh, thank you, but it's empty," Luigi replied. "But you're right, we should never litter in public buildings. Thank you." He picked up the envelope and left the building. It was very hot, but it did not bother him. A beggar, an Albanian, he thought, asked him for money, and Luigi gave him some loose change. Soon after that, a woman and her two children also asked for money and he gave her some change. On his way to the Duomo a third beggar approached him. Luigi pretended not to see him, and picked up his pace. He looked up at the pigeons flying about the Duomo and asked himself why on earth he wanted to go and live in the hills of the Marches. What was in store for him there? And in any case, where was it written that on reaching a certain age you have to welcome change ... especially when you have a new heart ...?

Chapter 24

Luigi left the bar at the Central Railway Station and headed for the train that would take him to Civitanova, in the Marches region. Before entering the area restricted to passengers only, he dropped his newspaper in the garbage. The lead story on the front had taken him by some surprise, though he half-expected it. Santamaria had killed himself, and his body was discovered in a local bar.

He had ventured into the bar in Via Manzoni the previous morning at around eleven, after their meeting. He had ordered a coffee and a mineral water and asked for the washroom. The waiter had handed him the key and a few minutes later heard a gunshot. With the help of some patrons he had smashed in the door and seen Santamaria's body slumped over the toilet, his eyes wide open, his face disfigured, an automatic gun on the floor and a large bloodstain on the wall behind the body. Santamaria had died by his own hand, like a scorpion that stings itself with its own tail when surrounded by fire. Luigi was not moved to pity at the news. He looked back from the window of the train and saw the great vault of the Central Railway Station getting smaller and smaller in the distance and thought that no one deserved to die, but least of all Valeria. He grabbed his suitcase, found a seat in a compartment and placed the suitcase on the overhead luggage rack.

That same morning at the Fatebenefratelli Hospital the doctor who removed his stitches had found him in good health, in spite of the insanity of travelling within ten days of bypass surgery. It was now time, the doctor had warned him, for a long period of rest. Luigi made no objection, partly

Between Rothko and 3 Windows

because he was tired, though not physically. An old friend was waiting for him at the Civitanova station. He would drive him up into those longed-for hills where he would stay for a while until he found the house of his dreams, some small peasant house in the middle of an orchard, where he would pass the time reading criminology manuals and maybe write a book or two, or three ... though in none of them would he touch upon this case.

A passenger seated across from him asked respectfully if it was OK to smoke. Luigi smiled, nodding his approval. The passenger lit up an MS, and Luigi took a deep breath, filling his lungs with the smoke that was rising to the ceiling.

What if the gun that killed Santamaria was the same one that had killed Beppe? No, that was impossible; the three of them killed Beppe. He should erase the past. The white wine in Petritoli would help him to forget. And if that was insufficient he would seek help from the *vincotto*.

Chapter 25

That afternoon the rain fell hard on the Comasina, pelting on the heaps of grey snow in and around the colonnade facing the piazza. You could buy anything at the Comasina, even the sun that had not been seen in days. There was a chaotic coming and going of addicts in the colonnade, but no sign of Beppe. Many looked like him, tall, thin, pock-marked, but he was nowhere in sight. We had circled the area for an hour, going as far as the shacks, where a half-dozen snotty kids were on the lookout for the cops. We had gone as far as Brezzo but found no trace of Beppe. We stopped at a bar for an espresso and within minutes of our sitting down were approached by all of our old friends who wanted to fence something, a camera, a scooter, a gold watch, drugs and so on, and so on. Finally an old schoolmate full of scabs and with hands swollen by too many needle marks panted inside the bar to tell us that Beppe could be found by the colonnade.

We hurried out and jumped in the car. We sat in silence, watching Raul drive nervously.

"Take it easy, Raul; we don't want to risk it with the cops," Michele said.

"Don't worry, we'll put this also on Beppe's tab," Raul replied.

We fell silent again. We stopped near the church, one of those neighbourhood churches built in the sixties to celebrate the popularity of cement. Raul wanted to wait in the car, but we convinced him that it was better for him to join us; otherwise the police would suspect something. The three of us left the car and headed for the colonnade. Someone with spent eyes stopped us, asking if we wanted to buy some stuff. Raul showed him the gun, and from that moment on no one dared bother us. Beppe was leaning against one of the pillars, half-asleep. He did not even notice we were there until Michele gave him a slap on his neck.

"What's up, Beppe?"

"Ah, Michele, it's you? What are you doing here?"

"What are you doing here, you prickhead?" Raul yelled out but was quick to lower his voice.

"What's with him?" Beppe asked, his eyes spent.

"Get a move on, you piece of shit!" Raul blurted.

"No," Beppe retorted. "I have things to look after."

"I'm going to ..." Raul hissed.

Michele grabbed Raul's arm, holding it back, while I approached Beppe and convinced him to follow us. We made for the car as quickly as we could, but Beppe insisted on stopping along the way to speak with small-time dealers. Finally he got into the car and sat beside me in the back just as Raul floored the engine angrily to get away from the Comasina. We took the bridge in the thick rain as darkness was falling. We stopped next to the cemetery. Raul turned off the engine, put it into second gear and turned to Beppe.

"You piece of shit! Why did you take the money?"

Beppe, who had fallen asleep with the cigarette in his mouth, opened his eyes and said in his plaintive nasal voice, "What the fuck are you talking about?"

"You know very well what I am talking about. You took the money, I counted it. Three million is missing. You bought a gram or two and had your own little party to mark the hit, you son of a bitch!" Raul shouted even more loudly.

Beppe was silent.

"Beppe, we had decided all together that we would not touch the money ... true or not? We decided not to touch it until the storm blew over, true or not?" Michele asked, turning on his seat to face Beppe.

"So who took it?" Beppe asked crossly.

"True or not?" Michele insisted, but there was no reply from Beppe.

Beppe's silence infuriated Michele, who was biting his lips as he kept on talking in a lower and lower tone of voice.

"You can't understand fuck all, that stuff is wasting you, idiot. We had promised ..."

Beppe woke up with a sudden jerk and started shouting. "You can all go fuck yourselves, yes, I used up the three million, so what? I made the hit, too! I was there too! It was my money!"

Raul lost all his self-control, turned around and took a closed-fist swing at Beppe's head. Michele tried to stop him, and Raul's fist landed on Beppe's nose while I moved away so I could kick Beppe in the ribs. He started vomiting as Raul pummelled him again on his ear. Beppe spit out a mixture of bile and blood.

Michele and Raul returned to their position and sat still, watching the rain pelting on the windshield. Night had fallen. I tried not to look at Beppe, who was whimpering against the window. Finally I handed Beppe a handkerchief. He wiped his nose.

"Even you, Tino? I expected it from them, but from you ..."

"What you did was really stupid, Beppe, big time stupid, and if the police catch you we are all done, you'll sell us out!" I told him, pushing his bloodied hands away.

"You're done with us," Michele said, without turning back, his gaze focused on the few cars splashing puddles on the highway, sending an explosion of droplets into the air.

"Is that so? Is that the way you thank me? I want my share!"

"You'll get it, then you get the fuck out!" Raul said.

"We're done with you, Beppe. You promised," Michele

said, cursing in a loud voice the stuff that had reduced Beppe to such a shred of a man.

"Let's go," Raul said, turning on the engine.

We took the road towards Bruzzano and drove to the hillside next to the bridge where they were building some condominiums. A few wooden shacks, used as storage sheds by farmers, dotted the landscape.

We stopped next to the metal barrier in a worksite and got out of the car. The rain had melted the snow into mud, and Raul, cursing, almost fell into it. I took Beppe by the arm and helped him walk. Raul sneered.

"So, it's over for real?" Beppe asked me, and I tried once again to avoid him.

"It's for your own good, and for ours. Until you stop with the stuff it's better if we share everything and go our own way," Michele said.

Beppe stopped, while the rest of us continued our climb on the hillside. Finally we all turned to look at him.

"I am not going anywhere, boys, I don't like this. Now you want to give me my share and only a moment ago you wanted to kill me," Beppe said in his plaintive voice, pressing the handkerchief to his ear.

We all looked at him. Raul shook the rain away from his trench coat. Michele approached Beppe, saying, "Idiot, don't you get it that it's better like this, we divide everything and we all disappear. You can do what you like." He turned around. "Let's go," he said.

Beppe stood there looking at us, befuddled, as we climbed the hill. Finally, like an abandoned puppy, he decided to follow us. Michele stopped at a shack and fished nervously in his rain-drenched pocket for the key to the lock. The keys fell; he cursed, looking for them in the mud till he found them and opened the door to the shack. We waited for him outside while he went in to look for the money. Beppe tried in vain to light up a cigarette. Michele came out and called everyone. The three of us approached the shack. Raul whispered in Beppe's ear as he took him over to the escarpment and suddenly pushed him over.

Beppe, who had fallen to the ground, struggled up. "No! Boys, don't leave me here," he shouted. "Take me with you. I understand, I'll stop, I swear I'll stop," he cried out. "Tino, you can help me, help me up. Tell those two that I won't do it anymore. Come on, boys, you know me ..."

I glanced over at Raul and Michele. No one said anything. Then Raul removed the gun from his belt, pointed it and took a shot, but the gun jammed. Beppe tried to run away, but he tripped and fell to his knees. His jeans were heavy with mud, his hair was drenched and he was bleeding profusely from the ear. "I get it, boys, I get it," he wept. "I've learned my lesson."

No one spoke. Michele took the first shot, followed by Raul. I took the last one. In the heavy rain it was difficult to tell I was weeping.

Chapter 26
July 3

"That's all of it." Luigi looked at Sergeant Stevens. "Everything that Tino Magnasco told me. By the time I left his house he was totally drunk and asleep with his head flat on the table. I gave him the rest of the money I had promised. I put it in his coat pocket, and I left."

Sergeant Stevens played with his ice cream spoon as Luigi looked on in silence.

"What's become of this Tino?" Sergeant Stevens asked.

"I guess he'll end up in jail. I don't want to know more about him, his life is already in ruins."

"So, our Michael Karrier, as it turns out, was hardly a saint ..."

Luigi struggled to agree. "He was no saint, but I never believed him, nor had Valeria Furlon. But she loved another man, a man who had changed."

"What about the money? What was it used for?"

"Beppe, Tino and Santamaria – Raul, just to be clear – had all grown up in the Comasina. Michele joined up with them, but he was from another area of Milan. Together they operated as a gang of young thieves. There were many such gangs in those days."

Luigi fell silent and turned to look out the window to College Street. It was still hot, but they were comfortable on the second floor of Bar Italia, which was on the shady part of the street. Luigi and Sergeant Stevens were the only guests. They felt safe as they nibbled at their gelato.

"Italy is such a great place," sneered Sergeant Stevens, even though Luigi was only half-listening to him. "At first they may have started stealing to get out of the ghetto, or maybe just for the money, but eventually they became radicalized and started sending money over to Lucio, the *torero*, to finance the guerrilla uprising, but it all went to rat shit when Beppe became a heroin addict. He started using stolen money to buy stuff, and soon enough the police would be on to him, putting everyone at risk. The only way out was to disappear from the scene, but for starters they would have to get rid of Beppe. In any case, was it Santamaria who dispatched the Peruvian?"

"Yes," Luigi said, searching in vain for a cigarette in his coat pocket. In his briefcase he had a stack of the copies of *Stampa Italica*, which he handed over to Sergeant Stevens. "These are all the articles I have written on the case, dating back to the day when Karrier was killed."

"This year, I promise, I will take a lesson or two of Italian. Would you like a beer?"

"No," Sasta replied. "You've forgotten that I have just had surgery? Lucio Marros, Raul and Michele had become good friends on their many trips to Peru, and when Santamaria told Lucio about Michele's intentions, he left for Toronto."

"Was the Peruvian a transvestite?"

"I don't know how he could pull the wool over my eyes."

"And Santamaria decided to have Michele killed after seeing him in Toronto?" Sergeant Stevens asked.

"After many years living in Toronto, Michele had returned to Milan, where he told Santamaria that he could no longer bear to live with his remorse, that justice should be served, that the truth about Beppe should come out. Santamaria took it badly, a violent argument ensued in their car and Santamaria made serious threats against Michele."

"How do you know all this?"

"From the horse's mouth. Once I was in his office, Santamaria told me everything. He knew I had spoken with Tino. Santamaria himself had given the photograph to Michele Carrieri many years before when he was in Toronto."

"And you, how do you feel?"

"Never felt better! I no longer smoke, I shouldn't eat so much," Luigi said in one breath.

"What's next ... retirement?"

"No, I'll wait for your call."

"You won't have to wait long; soon enough another Italian will end up killed."

"You old racist!" Luigi smiled and got up from the table.

"Where are you going?" Sergeant Stevens asked. "Come on, let's have a drink ..."

"I am meeting with Elena. Can you guess where?"

"The Art Gallery!"

"Exactly!"

"Just hang on a while longer, I have something to tell you." Sergeant Stevens took Luigi by his arm.

"What is it?"

"You have done an excellent job and have been of great help to me, especially since we've been able to wipe away this stain from our past."

"That's there to stay, Stevens, it will never go away; you can never outrun your past."

"I guess," Sergeant Stevens agreed. Luigi stood up again.

"Luigi?"

"Yes?"

"Why are you meeting your daughter at the Art Gallery?"

"We are going to look at one of Michele Carrieri's favourite paintings."

"But you've just told me this whole mess is over."

"Yes. It's really over, but I owe him. Listen? Can you hear it ... coming from outside?"

"What is it?"

"Everyone is getting ready for the game."

in red and green improvised a little dance. Luigi smiled, but he was at a loss to understand his unease among these festive people. A verse from the poem buzzed in his head. He could not understand why we cannot rebel against a life condemned to solitude: could it be due to a secret that could not be shared? He thought he finally understood the poem, just as he had understood the reason for the death of Michael Karrier. But it was clear that, while he could understand the mechanics of it, he could not accept Valeria's death, the brutality of it. Why did she have to die like that? He thought it banal to conclude that life is unfair, but Valeria had paid with her life for the finest of emotions, not for a "betrayal."

Aren't we all condemned to solitude? Luigi thought, as an older man threw his arms around him, babbling some nonsense about the game that was about to start. Even the drunks and the shouting fans with their heavy makeup were able to forget, if only for a moment, that the past is always with us; that the future looming before us is ready to pass us by, to become the ball and chain that slows us down, offering to become our only true lifetime companion. But perhaps no one was able to forget, only to take advantage of this festive distraction to put solitude at bay, if only for a while.

A man with a trumpet stepped out of a bar and blew a few dazed notes, much to the amusement of the crowd. In the trumpet blasts Luigi heard the grotesque hiccup that is the harbinger of death, saw the sobbing, bloodied bull fall to his knees, the sudden jerk of Michael Karrier. He saw Valeria. He took out from his wallet the sheet of paper on which he had copied the poem and which he had kept since the day of the murder at the Art Gallery and shredded it into tiny little squares which he threw into the noisy crowd in front of him.

They will think it is confetti, Luigi thought, picking up his pace to untangle himself from the crowd. I must have the Subaru fixed, no matter the cost. If they could fix me, and I am